THE
MINIATURE
MERMAID
ZENN(OF)OR

EMILY HARPER

CRANTHORPE
—MILLNER—
PUBLISHERS

First published by Cranthorpe Millner Publishers (2024)

ISBN 978-1-80378-163-1 (Paperback)

www.cranthorpemillner.com

Cranthorpe Millner Publishers

To my twin sister, who will forever be my little mermaid, and to my mother, who has fiercely believed in all of my wild dreams

'Though she be but little, she is fierce'

A Midsummer Night's Dream

CHAPTER 1

MONTY'S MINIATURES

Isla snuck between the crowds of roaming people sauntering up and down Portobello Road. The antiques market was bustling with traders and various customers in the Notting Hill borough of London. The dense air hummed with the sound of chattering voices: shouts coming from the market traders, perched behind their stalls; tourists cooing and talking in an array of languages, and locals meeting for their afternoon coffee. The market stall traders looked more like puppet masters than traders, selling everything you could possibly imagine, juggling and chattering. There were spice traders, jewellery sellers, antique dealers, souvenir stalls, cupcake stands, popcorn vendors and everything else anybody could think of.

It was a glorious day; the sun shone in the sky above London's streets, bathing the city in a delicious afternoon orange. London summers often felt overbearing and stifling to Isla, especially with the crowds in the city, but today was different. Today, she was on a very exciting mission. Isla was off to find her favourite market trader of all, Monty's Miniatures, which belonged to her grandad, Monty, who had some brand-new pieces to show her on his stall. Monty was a delightful man who had been selling his miniatures in Portobello market for over forty years. He had a strong Cornish accent from growing up in the West

2

Country and loved to chat about the weather, Cornish folklore and the price of food in London, so much so that people who visited his attractive stall would often get stuck in a conversation for several minutes, if not hours.

Monty always drew in a crowd with his impressive hand-made and tiny collectibles, which stood out amongst the other stalls on the busy market. Monty didn't make *all* his delicate pieces, for sometimes he would find a miniature at another antique market in a different part of the country and bring it back to sell it on his stall, alongside his own handcrafted pieces. Isla often stopped by to admire his delicate work, or browse his latest finds, on her way home from school. By four O'clock in the afternoon. during the week, the market was winding down, with the last few stragglers slowly packing away their wares. However, today was

Saturday, and the market was full to the brim.

Fortunately for Isla, she was small enough to move easily through the crowd, and as she made her way up the road, she could hear Monty's laugh bellowing in the distance. She smiled, wondering what magical miniatures he had to show her today. Isla weaved around a couple trying on peculiar hats, laughing and taking photos, and suddenly found herself right in front of his stall.

"Ello Isla!" called Grandad Monty, readjusting the spectacles that had slid down his nose. "Come to see my new miniatures have ya?" He chuckled and wove his arm in a swirling motion above his tiny items. "Plenty to choose from, my girl! Take a look but remember my one rule... use your imagination!" A hearty laugh erupted from his mouth and he winked playfully at Isla.

"Thanks Grandad Monty. Wow, they look beautiful." Isla shifted her eyes away from the miniatures. "Mum says I can't buy one this month, we can't afford it, even though I've been saving up my pocket money for weeks... but it doesn't matter." She turned back to look at her grandad and grinned. "I am so excited to see the new stock!"

Isla surveyed the breath-taking display before her. On the colourful table lay dozens of intricate miniature pieces: from tiny, elaborate bird cages – complete with fluffy birds made from real peacock feathers, to little figures of faeries with braided hair and woven, beaded skirts. Isla could spend all day admiring these ornate figurines.

As she gazed in delight, her hand found a figure covered in glittering, iridescent scales, so tiny and delicate they looked as if they could be real. She lifted the figure from beneath a piece of fallen fabric on the display. In her hand, the figure felt warm, and as she turned over the piece in her palm, she saw that it was a miniature mermaid. The skin on the miniature was smooth like silk, and the mermaid's flowing strands of hair were so fine they swished every time Isla moved the figurine. The miniature's delicate tail had fins that resembled those of a real fish, and Isla's mouth fell open as she carefully fanned the tail out with her fingertips. The mermaid's eyes were deep azure, like the Indian ocean, her lips were as bright as coral. How could this miniature appear so real?

Isla instantly fell in love with the tiny mermaid, and her heart danced as she sat in her palm. As a hobby, Isla collected any miniatures she could use in her tiny pirate cove, which she had recently made in her bathroom at home. Inside the cove was a miniature pirate with a swashbuckling cutlass, which pierced your skin if you touched it, along with a tiny dolphin with rubbery skin. The cove was made from rocks that she had collected from Hyde Park and shells from a family holiday back to Cornwall. Isla had made many miniature places over the years, including a tiny museum with mini dinosaurs, an Amazonian temple with miniature Mayans, a luscious vegetable garden with mini pumpkins and wheelbarrows, and a faerie wood full of tiny floating faeries, which she held up with fishing wire. But the pirate cove was by far her best work yet; it looked just like the Cornish coast.

Grandad Monty watched Isla assess the tiny figurine with satisfaction.

"She's a beauty that one. Found her in an antique dealer near Padstow – that's in Cornwall, my dear."

"Yes, I know Padstow, Grandad. We

went on holiday there..." Isla's voice trailed off dreamily as she watched the sun glimmer in the tiny mermaid's eyes. "Oh Grandad Monty, this tiny mermaid would fit perfectly into my little pirate cove! She looks so real... mermaids are at war with pirates, did you know?" Isla looked pleadingly at the old man, who sat on a stool behind his display of miniatures.

As he stood up, Monty made a wince and held his back with his hand for support. "Sitting' on them chairs all day does nothing for the old back!" He smiled awkwardly as he hobbled around the stall, crouching down to be face to face with his granddaughter.

"How much?" demanded Isla, eyeing Monty.

"Isla, you're my best customer," he declared confidently, pressing the miniature mermaid into her hand. "Take it, my dear. If you want her, she is yours."

Isla gazed up at Monty in amazement; she couldn't believe her ears. "But Grandad Monty, I have to give you some money..."

"No, I won't hear of it, my girl," Monty interrupted. "You take her and give her a good home now," he told her, ushering Isla along with a beaming smile.

"I will, I promise! She will be so happy in my pirate cove! Thank you, Grandad. See you later!" Isla waved the mermaid in the air as she was swept up by the crowd. She could see Grandad Monty waving from behind the shoulders of the people propelling her along the street.

With a sigh of relief, Isla managed to step onto the pavement and into an empty doorway to escape the bumbling pedestrians.

She looked down at the tiny mermaid and whispered, "Let's get you to your new home!"

With that, the mermaid went carefully into Isla's pocket for the duration of the walk home.

Once Isla was out of Portobello Road, the crowd thinned into little groups of people walking together, chattering in the afternoon sunshine. Isla took a left down a quaint side street where the houses were painted different shades of pastel blue, pink and yellow. Violet wisteria flowers tangled around the front of a powder blue house, where Isla lived with her mum. Rushing through the gate and along the path, Isla fumbled for her front door key, which she had been entrusted with to allow her freedom when her mum was working at home.

As Isla pushed open the wooden front door, light filtered into the dark hallway. Along the walls were framed photographs from her parent's adventures before she was born. Isla liked to look at these

10

pictures, noticing the exotic backdrops and smiling faces of two young adults, resembling her parents. The entire house was an eclectic mix of curiosities from around the world, collected by her parents when their work as travel writers took them to far flung corners of the Earth. These days, work was far harder to come by. Although her dad had written best-selling books and her mum still worked for a travel magazine as a journalist, money seemed to be a constant issue, and Isla had noticed the worry in her mum's eyes.

Isla's dad had been a handsome man, rugged and always in scruffy clothes from trekking up a far-flung mountain or exploring a hidden swamp in an unknown part of the world. But he had disappeared almost a year ago while working in Mexico and had never returned home. Isla missed her dad terribly, but she had to be strong to support her mum. Sometimes, Isla liked to imagine her dad's disappearance being explained by him secretly doing some vital research for a lost tribe in Africa or saving a whole ecosystem from invasion by a dastardly enemy in a jungle far away. The last communication that Isla and her mum had received was from Belize in Mexico – her dad's team had undertaken a diving expedition going after illegal shark poachers – but nobody had heard from him since, even after countless rescue missions, and her mum had stopped talking about him completely.

Isla kicked off her boots and walked down the hallway, up a small step at the end and into the kitchen. The kitchen had big glass windows which had replaced the wall between the kitchen and the garden, making it very bright; it seemed as if the garden was part of the interior of the house. The tiny, paved terrace was full of plants, and looked more like a little jungle than a city garden. Through the sparkling glass, Isla could see one of her miniature worlds: a tiny faerie kingdom, made from potted plants, rocks and two tiny faeries, one suspended in the air, making it look like it was flying right towards her.

From the kitchen cupboard, Isla took a large jug and filled it with water from the tap. Slowly, she spun around and walked back out of the kitchen, clutching the jug with both hands. She climbed the stairs in the hallway, taking great care not to spill any of the contents of the jug onto the floorboards. She wanted her little pirate cove to be just perfect, and pirate coves needed water. At the top of the stairs, Isla walked along the landing, padding softly in her socks, and pushed open a door at the end with her elbow. Inside the room she placed the jug atop of a chest of drawers, removed the miniature mermaid from her pocket, and placed her carefully onto the bed. Isla's room was full of little curiosities of her own; she loved to collect things just like her parents did. Trinkets from holidays and day trips to the coast decorated any available space in her bedroom. One day she was going to be a famous adventurer.

At the opposite side of the room to the door was another door, which led to a small bathroom, and this is where she had built her pirate cove. Isla had sacrificed her bathtub to make the little world of pirates and now... the pirates' enemy: rival mermaids. She looked inquisitively at the tiny, fierce pirate who stood at the helm of his mini ship, complete with tiny sails, decorated with the skull and crossbones.

Isla retrieved the miniature mermaid from the bed and carried her, along with the jug of water, carefully into her bathroom. With a steady hand, Isla filled the little cove she had made from rocks and shells with water, and placed the mermaid on the smoothest rock, with her tail coiled into a crescent, making her appear to have just leapt out of the water onto the rock to survey the cove and mock the pirate with her presence. Isla smiled with delight. Now the pirate cove was perfect!

"Isla, are you home?" came a lilting voice from the bottom of the stairs. The voice belonged to Isla's mum, who had been working in her study in the front room of the little house.

"I'm in my room, Mum. Look what Grandad Monty gave to me!" Isla replied excitedly.

Isla's mum appeared in the doorway of the bathroom and smiled at the sight of her daughter sitting on her knees beside the bathtub, beaming with delight.

"What *has* he given you now?" Isla's

mum asked, rolling her eyes in amusement and smiling back at Isla playfully. "He did say he had some new miniatures from Cornwall... would it be something to do with that, perhaps?" Isla's mum raised an inquisitive eyebrow in anticipation, letting her words linger for a moment.

Isla laughed and revealed the tiny mermaid, lifting her from her perch on the rock and delicately unfolding her in the palm of her hand.

"Oh Isla..." gasped Isla's mum "She is so beautiful... I can't believe it, she looks so real!"

"I know! I said I couldn't buy her, Mum, but Grandad Monty insisted I take her home with me. I didn't spend any money, Mum, really, I didn't." Isla's voice quivered with uncertainty. She didn't want her mum to be worried about money.

Isla's mum looked at Isla with a tilted

head and a crumpled expression on her face. "Isla, darling, it's okay. I want you to have toys, sweetheart, and Grandad likes to look after us. You know it brings him so much joy to see you happy. I think that's why he still spends every day on that little stall, hunting for things for you to enjoy."

The smile returned to Isla's mum's face and her focus drifted elsewhere for a second, outside of the room entirely. "Now then, what is her name?"

Both of them looked at the tiny face of the miniature doll.

"Actually Mum, I have no idea... what do you think?"

"I think her name will come to you eventually, best not to rush these things." Isla's mum kissed Isla on the top of the head. "Your little creation looks marvellous, sweetie; I am so proud of you! I wish I could be a little more creative sometimes. There just aren't enough hours in the day. Will you be okay if I do some more work, darling? There is so much to be done and Tony wants my article today, can you believe it? He only assigned it to me this week and Grandad wants to come for dinner... there is just too much to do!"

Isla liked that her mum talked to her as if she was responsible and grown up, but it was hard sometimes when she didn't know how to fix her mum's adult problems.

Isla's mum noticed the confusion on her daughter's face. "Oh, I am sorry darling, listen to me rambling on. Why don't you help Mummy and run to the shop to buy some groceries for dinner tonight? Grandad wants his favourite vegetable pie." Isla's mum rolled her eyes again.

"Of course, Mum, I know exactly what to buy, don't worry. I will be as fast as lightening!" Isla grinned. It made her feel better to be useful, knowing her mum was always so busy. This recipe had been in the family for generations. "I will roll out the pastry and get everything ready; it will be the best pie Grandad has ever eaten!"

"Thank you, sweetie. Money is on the hallway table" Isla's mum kissed her on the cheek and swished out of the room, her long black hair flowing behind her like a curtain.

Isla closed her bathroom door and pulled on her sweater. The long afternoon was coming to a close, and the sunshine of late summer was giving way to a slightly chillier early evening. In the hallway, Isla slipped on her trainers, took the £20 note from off the hallway cabinet, grabbed a wicker basket from the floor and skipped out of the front door.

The Saturday market was slowly winding down and groups of people were making their way to the Tube station, not far from the market. The row of small, terraced houses where Isla lived had become something of a tourist attraction; they were all painted different pastel shades and adorned with beautiful tangling wisteria. Rose bushes of many different varieties grew in the small gardens at the front of each house, making the little street look magically whimsical for inner city housing. Notting Hill felt like a little village in the heart of the West of London. Isla enjoyed living there, and loved having her Grandad Monty's flat just a few streets way from their home. Grandad Monty lived alone and his flat was a treasure trove of miniatures, antiques and trinkets from around Britain. He loved history and surrounded himself with anything that brought magic to his heart or a memory to his mind. Grandad Monty had an enormous imagination. Adults always say that only children have this gift, but Grandad Monty's imagination could swallow the world whole in its entirety.

CHAPTER 2

TALES FROM INSIDE THE KITCHEN CUPBOARD

Once inside the little grocery shop, Isla surveyed the vegetables on offer. She carefully chose a plump swede, three orange carrots – complete with green sprouting tops, a sumptuous pumpkin, a velvety red onion, a handful of garlic cloves and finally a sprig of fresh thyme. Grandad Monty loved her mum's vegetable pie because she made it exactly like Grandma Ivy, Isla's late grandma who had died before Isla was born.

The last of the market tourists crumpled into the open mouth of the underground railway, which flowed like pulsing veins through the city. Evening began to engulf the afternoon, bringing with it cool, gentle breeze. Isla skipped home from the grocery shop and pushed open the front door. She could hear her mum winding down her last phone conversation of the day. Softly, Isla closed the door and whizzed to the kitchen. The afternoon light beamed through the glass windows, making dust bunnies dance in the air. Isla pulled a chair from beneath the big, wooden table and pushed it towards a cupboard in the corner of the kitchen. Standing carefully on one leg, she reached up like a ballet dancer into the cupboard and felt around for a big leather book: 'Tales of Zennor'. Inside this book were recipes, tales and memories from Grandma Ivy. Although she had never met her, Isla felt that she knew her from this time capsule. Her grandma's voice spoke out through the words on the pages and Isla felt a warm glow in her heart every time she read the inscriptions.

Isla turned carefully to her grandma's recipe for 'Magic Vegetable Pie'. Grandad Monty always said that the magic came sprinkled from Grandma Ivy's smile. Humming to herself, Isla began to flick through the pages of the heavy, worn-out book. On each page were sketches, scribbled captions and songs springing from the page and dancing around Isla's imagination. Isla began to wobble on her chair and quickly steadied herself. She knew her mum didn't like it when she let her imagination take over her body. Grandad Monty always said that Isla was a girl with her head permanently in the clouds... whatever that meant.

"Isla! Get down, please." Isla's mum entered the kitchen and her eyebrows almost raced upward completely off her forehead, upon seeing Isla balancing on a chair, holding the precious book aloft.

Isla wobbled with a start and her mum rushed to steady her. Isla passed her mum the heavy book and jumped down off the chair sheepishly.

"Sorry, Mum. I wanted to help..." Isla beamed with enthusiasm.

"I know, sweetheart, but please be careful. Grandad's book is very precious to him, and you are very precious to me, so please try not to destroy both of those things in our kitchen..."

The book now sat proudly on the wooden work surface, and Isla's mum began to hum a tune as she prepared their dinner. Isla noticed a folded piece of paper that had fallen out of the book and onto the floor. The paper was crumpled and worn. She carefully unfolded the paper to see what was written.

The Ballad of The Mermaid of Porthzennor Cove

She swims through the current,
But walks onto shore,
Her eyes are dazzling sapphires,
Beware of this creature: do not adore.

From the depths of the ocean,
She is pulled to the people of Zennor.
To St Senara's Church she wanders,
Where waits a man with a harmonious tenor.

Maybe a look, perhaps a slight touch,
She entices Matthew with a spell.
He cannot resist the pull of the waves,
Off he strides to the ocean, his mind a closed shell.

Underneath the poem was a faded photograph of what looked like a bench with a mermaid carved into the side, looking down on the ocean with great authority. Isla scratched her head in confusion. Why had her grandad never told her about this poem before? They had looked through this book together so many times. Next to the picture of the bench was a hand drawn arrow and the label 'St Senara's Parish, 1509'. Then, underneath this, a strange rhyme was scribbled:

'When the song is done, the seahorses will bow, and you shall be one.'

Isla remained confused and re-read the beautiful poem. Some of the words did not make much sense, but she knew it was a clue to something very important.

Suddenly, a voice came from behind her shoulder.

"Where... where did you... you get that?"

Isla spun round with a jump and saw Grandad Monty peering over her shoulder, his hand supporting his arched back.

"Grandad! You scared me." The old man tended to sneak up on her; he thought it was hilarious to play tricks on his granddaughter. Isla disagreed. She thought it was very annoying.

With a chuckle, Grandad Monty lifted the paper out of her hand, his eyes scanning the page and his mouth slightly open. "Isla, where on Earth did you find this? This page was ripped out years ago, it is bad luck..."

His eyes glazed over, and Isla noticed his usual twinkle had disappeared.

"I think it fell out of the book, Grandad, I don't know where it came from. I took the book from the cupboard and then I just found it on the floor." Isla pointed to the book on the counter, which was turned to the recipe page.

At that moment, the sound of clattering pots and pans interrupted their conversation, and after some muffled complaining and more clattering, Isla's mum appeared from the utility room.

"That blasted cupboard. I never find the time to organise it and..." She trailed off, suddenly noticing Grandad Monty. "Dad! You're early! Come and sit down, you shouldn't stand like that; you work all day in cold weather on that silly stall... out in the elements all day long, it's not good for your health..." Isla's mum ushered Grandad Monty towards the table and chairs, supporting his arm all the way. Grandad Monty winked at Isla, who stood watching the scene with a raised eyebrow. Isla always thought it was strange that her mum fussed so much over Grandad Monty; he was packed to the brim with energy and vitality, more so than any other person Isla had ever met!

"What's wrong with you two?" asked Isla's mum suspiciously, noticing the exchange of looks between Isla and Grandad Monty. She always had a way of reading unsaid words in a room.

"Well, Isla found something in that old book over there. Show your mam, girlie!" Grandad Monty's finger jabbed the air towards the paper as Isla's mum pushed a walking stick into his hand.

Isla brought the paper to her mum and watched as she scanned the page. For a second, her mum's eyes widened, and Isla thought she saw her exchange a concerned look with Grandad Monty, which Isla couldn't decipher. But before she could blink, her mum's expression went back to normal.

"I don't know why you two are acting so strange about it. Honestly, Dad, you look like you've seen a ghost! It's just another poem from that book, it probably fell out because the binding is so old..." Her voice trailed off as she noticed the boiling pot overspilling.

Grandad Monty shrugged and beckoned Isla over to the table. "Come and sit with your old pal," he said.

"Some of us have to make dinner, Grandad," replied Isla in a lofty tone, glancing to check if her mum had heard her.

"Why don't the two of you make yourselves useful and tidy that old book away." Isla's mum slammed the book on the table in mock annoyance. "I've finished with the recipe anyway."

"Don't listen to your mother, Isla, this book holds all the stories from where you come from, my girl. It's not all myths and

31

legends, you know." Grandad Monty raised his voice slightly at the end so that Isla's mum could hear, though she just flipped her hair and ignored him. Grandad Monty carefully opened the old front cover and the pages hinged like the creaking of a door. Grandad slipped the old poem back inside. "Best keep that safe." He winked.

CHAPTER 3

A SEA CHANGE...

Isla, her mum, and Grandad Monty sat around the table, smiling at the bubbling, golden pie before them in the centre.

"Okay, time for Magical Vegetable Pie," announced Isla's mum with a beaming smile, her shoulders starting to relax for the first time that day.

"Bravo!" boomed Grandad Monty, his eyes twinkling with expectation as he eyed the delicious pie he had been waiting all day to taste. "There ain't nothing like the taste of a magical pie to keep an old man on his feet."

Isla's mum started dishing out the steaming pie onto plates. The bright evenings were slowly fading as autumn drew near, and the pie was a gentle heat in the cooling kitchen. Fairy lights and candles lit up the room, strung from Isla's mum's numerous cookery books. Behind the glass doors, where the tiny garden lay, solar lights hung in lanterns on the old brick walls and in the flowerpots. Isla could see her miniature faerie world in the twinkling lights. Saturday evenings when Grandad Monty came over were Isla's favourite part of the week. Grandad Monty always brought stories with him and the three of them would sit around the kitchen table, listening and talking until very late at night. Isla would go to bed exhausted but enthralled by the mystery of her grandad's tales.

"How about a song?" suggested Grandad Monty after they had finished dinner.

"I heard thee sing in the church above
the ocean,
I heard thee sing, my pretty boy.
Far from my jaunty palaces,
I have come to thee, my pretty boy."

Isla smiled at the old song and her mum laughed, rolling her eyes. Another strange look was exchanged between the pair, but Isla still couldn't work out what silent conversation they were having.

"Come on, Dad! That's enough now. Have you had your medication yet?" Isla's mum rested a hand on Grandad Monty's arm as he banged the table to punctuate the lyrics in the old sea shanty.

"Medication? Do I look like a man in need of medication?" smiled Grandad

Monty, eventually rolling his eyes. "Yes, Imogen, I have taken my medication. Sometimes you act like the old person around here..."

Isla's mum frowned slightly and patted Grandad Monty's hand. "Just making sure, Dad. We have to look after each other, especially since Dan..." her voice trailed off, as if she was paralysed by the sound of Isla's dad's name.

Isla didn't understand why nobody ever talked about her dad anymore. She lowered her eyes, feeling a little sad.

Isla's mum shook herself back to the present. "Isla, Grandad and I have something we need to talk to you about..."

Isla noticed yet another exchange of looks between her mum and Grandad Monty.

"Okaaay..." encouraged Isla with slight trepidation. Something felt wrong, like they were going to tell her bad news, or that she had to go to bed early.

"Well, you know how money has been a bit tight recently, darling? Well... sometimes it just isn't there... and London is so very expensive, it costs a lot of money, and with your dad missing... it just can't go on like this." Isla's mum's voice faltered slightly. "We have decided that it might be, or will be, better to start a new life outside of London... in... Cornwall."

"What?" Isla blurted out in shock, not expecting this news. "How long have you been secretly planning my life behind my back? What about me? What about my school? My friends? Grandad?" Isla could feel burning tears of anger rising and she let them overflow, dripping onto the table.

"Oh Isla, darling, please don't be upset. This will be so good for us! All of us need a break from this city. I know you have friends here, but you will make new friends! You are so young, sweetie... oh, and Grandad, Grandad will be coming with us Isla!"

Isla's mum looked at Grandad Monty with panic in her eyes, silently begging him for support.

"Come now, Isla, dry your eyes. It'll be an adventure! I'm getting too old to be sitting' on that stall all day. I need to go back to the fresh Cornish air, the rolling hills, the lush meadows, the crooked woods, the tiny fishing villages... ah... I can see it now..." Grandad Monty's voice trailed off as his mind drifted.

Isla still snuffled, wiping her tears with her hands. She couldn't look at either of them. How dare they sit around this table, in her home, suggesting that they should give up everything!

"What about Dad, hm? Did you think about that in your grand plan? How will he find us again if we leave?" Isla announced, staring directly at her mother in defiance.

"Isla, your dad... Daddy isn't coming home, sweetie. He's been gone too long, you know that don't you? It's... it's just the three of us now." Isla's mum choked on her own unshed tears. "Sorry, I... I just need a moment." She stood abruptly, knocking her leg against the table as she left the room in a hurry.

Isla knew she was going to cry in the bathroom, and she suddenly felt very guilty. Grandad Monty smiled meekly at Isla and pulled a handkerchief from his trouser pocket. He always had a handkerchief.

Slowly, he wiped the tears now trickling from her eyes, humming a folk tune softly. Isla eventually stopped crying, listening to the melody of her grandad's voice.

"Grandad, is Mum okay?" Isla asked delicately, as if the words had crept from beyond her lips without her permission.

"Your mum will be okay, pal, she just

needs a bit of a break."

Isla's anger began to calm, and a tiny seed of thought grew in her mind; perhaps Cornwall wouldn't be so bad. After all, she had always enjoyed holidays there, and Mum was happier by the sea. They were all happier by the sea.

Grandad Monty stood from his chair with a groan, leaning against the table as he reached for his stick. "I'll go check on your mum, make sure the old girl's okay." He shuffled slowly towards the kitchen door and left the room, the door creaking behind him.

Isla stood up and went to the big glass window, to peer into the foliage beyond in the garden. She let her breath fog the glass in front of her and drew a sad face with her index finger. There, in the corner, was her miniature faerie kingdom, made with Grandad Monty's tiny figures and plant pots. It was well known amongst the

Cornish folk that faeries lived in the forests and wildflower meadows; there were many folk tales which Grandad Monty had told Isla time and time again. Isla began to let her imagination expand into the garden and over the London streets, soaring deep into the night sky, winding its way down to the South-West. If Cornwall was good enough for faeries, then it was good enough for her!

Isla saw in the reflection of the glass that her mum had slipped back into the room, with Grandad Monty hobbling behind her.

"Hi darling, sorry about that. Mummy just needed the bathroom."

Her mum's voice was soothing and calm, but Isla could see that her eyes were red and a bit puffy. Isla walked over slowly and put her arms around her mum, burying her face into her mum's clothes, which always smelled like home. She

41

could feel her mum soften in the embrace as she stroked Isla's head slowly to comfort her; it was something she had done since Isla was a baby and it always stole away her anxiety. It was them against the world and they were going to make it work.

Grandad Monty had sat back down in his chair and was flicking through the Book of Zennor at the table. "Come and sit," he said. "Let's have a story."

CHAPTER 4

THE MERMAID OF ZENNOR

Grandad Monty cleared his throat as Isla's mum lit another candle on the table. Mother and daughter cuddled up together on the bench, wrapped in blankets ready for the old folk tale, and so Grandad Monty began...

"It was a cold, wintery evening in the depths of December. St Senara – an old, medieval church – sat proudly in the centre of a tiny village named Zennor. The village sat in between St Ives and St Just, nestled on the perilous north-west coast, where the Atlantic Ocean meets the

Cornish coastline. The ancient doors of the church rattled in the wind as the evening service began. Within the church, a man named Matthew sang in the rectory at the head of the choir. It is said that his singing voice could lure angels from the heavens to sit amongst the congregation. Aye, it was a sweet sound indeed, for a stranger had heard the melodies and come to search for the origin of the sound.

"At the back of the church, lit only by candlelight – they didn't have light switches in them days – the heavy, gnarled doors to the church creaked open, revealing the stranger against the starry night sky. A gust of wind blew down the centre aisle, extinguishing each candle one by one. The parishioners gasped in unison, for they had never seen this strange woman before. The lanterns on the walls remained lit and an amber glow encircled the stranger's face as she glided through the entrance to take a seat. It is said that the beauty of the woman's face was like no other. Eyes, like turquoise crystals; straight from the purest of oceans. Her skin was white like porcelain and as delicate as a flower petal; her lips were as pink as coral from a tropical reef and her hair cascaded down her back, swishing as she walked, silver in the light and curled in soft waves. The woman appeared like a vision from another world. Nobody could believe their eyes. Despite the pouring rain, the woman's intricate black dress was dry, and her flowing hair remained without a single droplet of water.

'Please,' said the mysterious woman, 'do not stop singing, I want to listen.'

Shocked by the woman's entrance and stunned by her mesmerising voice, which danced out of her lips, Matthew finished his song, to the amazement of the congregation. The woman took a seat in one of the wooden pews at the back of the church, her eyes fixed on the singing man. She did not blink or look at any other face in the church. The congregation resumed their service and the strange woman's presence was accepted at the back of the church. At the end of the service, the woman stood to leave, her dress flowing behind her. Matthew hurried to the back to try and stop the woman before she left. He was unsuccessful; the woman had vanished.

"But that was not the end of our mysterious tale... for the woman returned; night after night she took the same seat at the back of the church, focusing only on Matthew as he sang chorales in the candlelight. Nobody had ever spoken to the stranger, as she always arrived late and left early. One day, the woman arrived just as the service began, and

46

Matthew was waiting at the back of the church, ready for her to enter. The organist lumbered on with a tune at the front of the church as the woman started with a fright on seeing Matthew behind the door.

'Please Miss, I do not mean to frighten you, but I must know your name... please, would you oblige me this one precious courtesy?'

'Morveren,' whispered the woman. 'My name is Morveren.'

'You are the most beautiful woman I have ever seen. Please tell me where you come from...' Matthew trailed off, falling deep into the tiny oceans that swirled in the woman's eyes.

'I am from a world of magic, far more captivating than you could ever imagine...' replied the woman, holding Matthew's gaze. 'Would you like to come with me? If you do, you can never return.'

"Spellbound by the woman, Matthew followed her out into the starry night. The couple walked down onto the moonlit beach, in Porthzennor Cove, where the waves crashed relentlessly against the shore. The woman walked soundlessly into the ocean and dove beneath the freezing waves. Awe struck, Matthew simply followed her, and was never seen again.

"In memory of their beloved Matthew, and the mysterious stranger who had captured his heart, the parishioners of St Senara church carved the image of a mermaid onto the wooden bench where the strange woman always sat, in the hope that one day she would return with Matthew to St Senara. To this day, the bench still sits at the back of the old church in the village of Zennor, waiting for its tenant to return... It is known by all who live there as 'The Mermaid's Chair'."

"Bravo Grandad!" cheered Isla in the candlelight of the kitchen.

Grandad Monty snapped the book shut for dramatic effect. "And that, my dear girl, is how ye tell a tale!" He chuckled. "This old book has life in her yet!".

Isla's mum yawned and wriggled from beneath the blanket. "Just like the man reading it." She smiled.

"Grandad, St Senara is the church drawn on the bottom of that poem I found earlier, on that piece of paper... that's the mermaid chair, from the photograph..."

Grandad Monty simply gave Isla a wry grin in response.

"Right my darling, it's time for you to get some rest, and time for Grandad to get off home before it gets too late," said Isla's mum, clapping her hands together.

"Mum, I think Cornwall will be a wonderful change," smiled Isla.

Her mum beamed, and gave her the

biggest hug she could.

The two climbed the stairs to Isla's room after Isla had kissed her grandad goodnight. Her mum crouched to switch on Isla's star shaped night light as Isla pulled on her pyjamas and wriggled beneath the duvet. The little star shaped night light glowed, and Isla imagined the lanterns from the story.

"Mum, do you believe in magic?" asked Isla sleepily.

"Isla, the world is full of magic, you just need to know where to look..."

With that, Isla's mum kissed her daughter on the forehead and softly walked out of the room, pulling the door to on her way out. Isla turned over in her bed and let sleep take her into a world of dreams, where folk tales came to life and mermaids swam through the seven seas, weaving magic into the waves and singing out to the sea creatures as they slept in the blue-green depths.

CHAPTER 5

A FINAL FAREWELL

The next few weeks were a whirlwind of packing, organising and rearranging. Isla helped her mum put the entire house into boxes; all of their precious books, artefacts and memories were shut away between layers of cardboard. This seemed very strange to Isla, and she often felt worried and unsure of what was to come. Throughout the house, boxes were piled high with black scrawled writing along the sides naming the contents within; Isla hadn't realised their whole house could be packed away into tiny capsules of cardboard. She had left her mermaid cove in the bathroom for as long as possible – she didn't want to disturb her little world until absolutely necessary – but she knew she would need to pack it all away soon. Still, her mum seemed brighter and happier in the days leading up to the big move, so that made Isla feel a little better.

Grandad Monty had managed to reduce his entire London flat, which was a treasure trove of things, to a small truckload of little suitcases, furniture and boxes. The house they were moving to was an old farmhouse and Grandad Monty would have his own room and bathroom at the back of the house. Isla had seen a photograph of the house, and of her room, which was a lot bigger than her room in Notting Hill. On the day of the move, a huge lorry turned up at the house, squeezing down the tiny lane where their house sat sandwiched between the other little terraces. Four men carried out all of the furniture and boxes one by one like a human conveyor belt, emptying the house like clockwork. Soon, all that was left was the peeling wallpaper and scuffed carpets, like a skeleton being revealed.

Isla stood in the doorway of the house once everything had been removed. A small tear trickled down her face as memories of all the happy years spent growing up in this house and this city replayed in her head. Isla's mum came walking up to join her in the doorway and the pair looked at each other. No words were needed; they simply hugged each other hard and shed more tears for all the happy memories they were leaving behind. Holding hands, they walked down the path to where Grandad Monty stood against the gatepost, a huge grin on his face.

"Come on you two! This is going to be exciting, you're like two wailing cats over there," he called over to them, banging his stick on the floor.

They all laughed tentatively, despite the tense atmosphere. Isla felt overcome with emotions that she didn't quite understand; she just knew that she needed to be as close to her family as possible. Grandad Monty had already sent his truck of belongings down to the farmhouse in Zennor, so all that was left to do was to close and lock up their Notting Hill home one final time, shutting the memories and her life so far inside. The removal van ambled off like an old elephant down the street and the family watched it turn off Portobello Road and into their future; they would meet the lorry in Cornwall.

This is it... it's really happening, thought Isla, staring blankly at her old front door.

Her whole body felt tingly and strange, as if she were leaving part of herself behind.

Isla's mum helped Grandad Monty into the front passenger seat of their car and he winced as he flopped into the seat, which bounced slightly beneath him as he settled. Isla closed the door and watched her mother jump into the driver's seat, wiping her eyes as she turned the key in the ignition of the old Land Rover. Isla took one final look at the old market, watching as the first of the traders began to set out their stalls. She saw the street now as if it were stuck in a moment of time. This market, this street would be forever here, but Isla knew she had big adventures to come in Cornwall. She smiled sadly and tapped her pocket where her miniature mermaid lay patiently waiting for her new home.

"Right! Let's blow this market stall," cried Grandad Monty, clapping his hands and grinning in the rear-view mirror.

Isla's mum made a snivelling sound and shook her head, revealing a small smile. "Too right, Dad. Onwards and upwards, as they say." With this proclamation, she pressed on the accelerator and off they motored down the street, dodging tourists and commuters on their way to the motorway that would remove them from the city.

Grandad Monty hummed a wordless sea shanty, his lilting song descended into the air, as Isla watched the road ahead being gobbled by their car. Grandad Monty reached awkwardly behind into the back of the car and handed Isla a photograph of a big stone house, covered in plants and flowers, nestled in the dip of a rolling hill. In the garden of the house, she could see neat vegetable patches and smoke coming from a chimney on the roof. The weather was grey, but bright tones descended on the vegetation, as if gaps in the clouds masked a brilliant light, allowing shards to descend in fragments.

"So, which room will you have pet?" asked Grandad Monty in is usual bright tone. Nothing ever phased him; he had an amazing ability to only see good things and to only say good things too. He always made Isla feel happy and relaxed, even in not so good situations. When her dad had disappeared, it was Grandad Monty who had organised everything in their lives, right down to dinner when her mum couldn't get out of bed and Isla had felt like she was making everything worse because every time she asked a question her mum burst into tears. Grandad Monty never cried and he always tried to answer her questions, even if he didn't always know the right answer. Her mum was much happier now and Isla didn't feel so confused, but she still missed her dad every day and knew he was just waiting somewhere so he could return. She was sure everything would be explained, and they would all laugh about it soon enough.

"I will have the biggest room!" proclaimed Isla. "I need somewhere I can put all of my miniature worlds, and the mermaid cove, though maybe I'll put that in the garden this time..." Isla's imagination started whirling. Where would she put everything?

"Don't worry darling, this house has a lot more space than the old one," chimed Isla's mum, looking much brighter than before.

"This house is full to the rafters with magic, mark my words girl, you will be astonished soon enough."

Isla's eyes grew wider as her grandad continued.

"You see, I grew up in the house we're moving to, and when I was a lad I saw faeries in the garden, and little sprites in the rooms. Me mam thought I were telling lies but I can tell you that I know what I saw."

Isla gasped in astonishment.

"Well Dad, I have been many times to the house, and I have never seen a faerie, so don't fill Isla's head with promises. We need to settle in properly. When I'm there, I just feel very relaxed; it's so peaceful, Isla. At night, the only sound you can hear is the ocean beyond the fields. Sometimes, when I wake up there, I just want to spring out of bed and into the garden to sing at the top of my lungs." Isla's mum smiled indulgently.

"That's great, Mum." Isla smiled into the rearview mirror, catching her mum's eye in the reflection.

Meanwhile, Grandad Monty had closed his eyes and was leaning against the windowpane, fast asleep. Isla decided to do the same; it was very early in the morning after all, and her mum had said they would stop somewhere just after Bristol for some lunch. The journey to Zennor would take them hours and Isla already felt exhausted. With the countryside flashing past them on all sides of the car, she closed her eyes, allowing sleep to relax her muscles and calm her mind.

CHAPTER 6

ALL ROADS LEAD TO ZENNOR

"WHAT SHALL WE DO WITH THE DRUNKEN SAILOR!"

A booming voice shattered Isla's dreams of mermaids, waking her from a very deep sleep.

"Grandad!" shouted Isla, startled and confused.

Grandad Monty stood next to the car with the door open, a wicked grin on his face. Isla could feel a chilly breeze filling the vehicle.

"You didn't think I would let me old pal sleep through lunch, did ya? OOOH...

WHAT SHALL WE DO WITH THE DRUNKEN SAILOR..." Grandad Monty continued singing loudly, attracting looks from the other travellers milling about the car park.

"Shh, please Grandad, people are staring. They'll think you're mad," mumbled an embarrassed Isla, cringing and shrinking deeper into her seat.

"Well then I shall have accomplished my mission... always wanted to be a crazy old grandad," chuckled Grandad Monty, still not lowering his voice.

He never cared what people thought of him and his silly songs, which Isla quite admired in a funny sort of way.

"Come on you, up you get. Yer mum's inside the service station buying coffee, let's go and stretch our legs."

Isla uncrumpled herself from her seat and hopped out of the car, her weight collapsing under a dead leg. "Oomph," she groaned as she hopped after Grandad

Monty, closing the car door behind her. There were a lot of people cramming into the service station.

"Last of the summer stragglers," said Grandad Monty, as if he could read her mind. "Brings all the ants out of the colony," he whispered as they walked slowly into the service station, dodging parents with pushchairs and children darting about in all directions.

Through the crowds, Isla's mum became visible at the coffee counter. She was gesturing to the lady behind the counter, who looked bemused. On seeing the two stragglers, she immediately rushed over.

"What do you two want to drink? Apparently, they don't have almond milk here... can you believe it? I'll have to have black coffee instead. Dad?"

Grandad Monty looked wide eyed and simply said, "Yes dear, whatever you have

I'll have the same..."

"Mum, can I have a Frappalicious with marshmallows and syrup?" pleaded Isla.

"I'll ask sweetie, but don't get your hopes up, we're in Cornwall now," replied her mum, glancing back at the confused lady at the coffee counter.

Isla was excited; she couldn't believe they were in Cornwall already! Her mum must have decided to just keep driving while she and Grandad Monty napped, rather than stopping off in Bristol. Isla took another look around her. *This is where we live now*, she thought. *From today, I'll be Cornish, just like Grandad.*

Once she and Grandad Monty had visited the bathrooms, they returned to find Isla's mum balancing three drinks on a cardboard tray and looking rather flustered. She shoved the drinks into their hands.

"No Frappalicious, Isla, so you have a

strawberry milkshake with clotted cream. Let's go and sit on that bench there and eat something." Isla's mum gestured wildly towards the last available bench outside, which was being rapidly approached by another family.

"Go on Isla!" Grandad Monty gave her a little push and she ran off ahead of her family to secure the bench.

Isla flopped herself down just before one of the other family's children manged to get himself sat down. She smiled a beaming smile and shrugged her shoulders.

"Sorry, I was here first," she cooed in delight. Isla knew Grandad Monty needed a seat, even if he proclaimed that he didn't over and over again.

The boy frowned at her with a terrible glare and held his ice cream over her head. "If you don't move, I'll drop this on you!"

Isla looked up at the boy in shock and searched frantically for her family. Suddenly, out of the crowd, came Grandad Monty, hobbling quickly on his stick over to the bench.

"Oi! Get lost you rascal," shouted Grandad Monty from ten paces away, waving his stick precariously in circles near his head. He almost hit a teenager with headphones attached to her ears; the girl had to duck beneath the stick to avoid getting thumped.

The boy grinned wickedly as Grandad Monty approached. "You don't scare me, silly old man. You can't even walk!" The boy stuck his tongue out at Grandad Monty before laughing and marching back to his family.

"What a nasty little lad," remarked Grandad Monty, still staring in the direction of the boy and making his voice slightly louder. "You okay, Isla?" he enquired, looking her over as he pulled out his handkerchief.

"I'm okay, thanks Grandad. Is everybody like that down here?" Isla asked anxious, watching with wide eyes as the boy kicked his younger brother and cackled wildly.

"No, my pet, he's just a silly bully, and there aren't many of those in Zennor, mark my words."

Grandad Monty shook his head as Isla's mum came into view, holding a huge picnic basket in one hand and their drinks in the other.

"Oh, don't worry about me you two, I'll just do everything, shall I?" Isla's mum had evidently been back to the car to fetch their lunches, and was struggling to carry everything.

Isla jumped up and rescued her mum just as she was about to drop her coffee.

"Thank you, sweetie," said Isla's mum.

"Always Mummy's helper."

Isla smiled, though she didn't particularly like it when her mum said that – it made her feel babyish – but she decided to allow it just this once.

Isla's mum had made a wonderful effort with their little picnic. Inside the basket, lined with a strawberry print cloth, were delicious jam sandwiches, plump raspberries, Isla's favourite salt and vinegar crisps and freshly baked scones. The family wrapped themselves up in their coats and tucked into the treat.

"Well done, Immy," praised Grandad Monty through a mouthful of scone. "You know I love a jam scone, me."

Isla's mum nursed her coffee in both hands. She looked a little tired. "Is everybody warm enough?" she fussed. "We can sit in the car, I just thought it might be nice to get some fresh air, you know?".

"It's great Mum!" said Isla, through mouthfuls of sticky jam sandwich.

"Legend has it, when you cross through the gateway to Cornwall, you have to say hello to the mermaids and the faeries." Grandad Monty winked, grabbing another scone.

Isla giggled as her mum rolled her eyes. The service station began to quiet down as everybody packed back into cars and continued their journey out of Cornwall.

"Glad that throng of tourists has gone," remarked Grandad Monty with a superior tone in his voice. "Wild lot they were, wild lot indeed..." He glared at the boy with the ice cream who was being rounded up into a packed car full of his brawling siblings. He was sticking his tongue out in their direction.

Isla's mum followed his gaze towards the car with a confused frown on her face, then looked back at Grandad Monty, who stuck his own tongue out at the boy in return.

"Right, Dad, anyway... we should get going soon, else we'll be here for hours. I promise it's much nicer in the village than sat here at the service station. Let's go." Isla's mum packed away their little picnic, and before long, everybody was back in the car.

As they drove, the big, busy roads gave way to winding little paths that snaked through the countryside, all guarded by hedge soldiers. It wouldn't be long until Isla would be able to see the sea and hear the beating waves crashing onto magical shores.

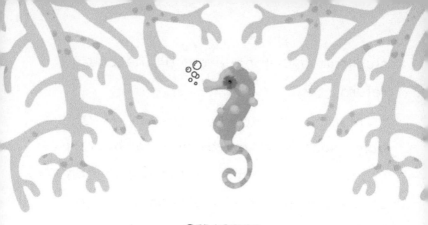

CHAPTER 7

WELCOME TO CORNWALL!

As the car rolled over the crest of a hill, Isla caught sight of the ocean in all its shades of blue. The body of water sprang up from the horizon like a giant blanket being unrolled, and it wasn't clear where the ocean ended and the sky began. White topped waves lapped against the sand and rock, arranged in crescent, jagged bays. The sea felt wondrous and awe inspiring. Although Isla had been to Cornwall as a child, she didn't remember feeling this excited. Grandad Monty had continued his stories of mermaids, faeries and magical creatures for the last hour, and even Isla's mum was beginning to relax.

The car turned inland from the ocean and down a smaller road. The road swivelled and wound around tiny streams and through dense woodland. Eventually, they came to an ancient church in the centre of a quaint little village. Isla gasped at the tiny cottages scattered around the church, their gardens filled with beautiful flowers. scattered around the hedgerows. The car continued through the village as Grandad Monty went into full director mode, bossing Isla's mum with directions and making hand signals for her to follow.

"And this, ladies, is Zennor!" boomed Grandad Monty, throwing his hands in the air dramatically, almost hitting Isla's mum in the face as she leaned forward to check the condition of the road ahead.

"Oh, will you calm down, Dad? Honestly,

it is like having two children in the car. Isla is more grown up than you! I need to concentrate; the road isn't smooth and I don't want to get stuck in the mud..." Isla's mum trailed off as she concentrated once more on the road ahead.

Grandad Monty pretended to sit up properly in his seat with a straight back, closed an invisible zip on his mouth and clasped his hands in his lap, looking at Isla's mum mischievously out of the corner of his eye and winking at Isla in the rearview mirror. Isla let out a tremendous laugh then clamped her hand over her mouth; this made Grandad Monty roar with laughter and then eventually Isla's mum joined in, her chest heaving with giggles as she tried to focus on the uneven road.

The family continued up a little track and over a tiny bridge, where a brook trickled through brambles. Eventually, the road opened up, and Isla could see the magnificent farmhouse for the first time in the distance. The house looked exactly like the photographs and Isla jumped up and down in her seat with excitement.

"There she is, the old beauty," Grandad Monty beamed. "I think we are going to be very happy here."

Isla nodded frantically, squeezing the miniature mermaid in her pocket. She had almost forgotten about her; she would be back in her cove soon enough.

The car came to a stop on the gravel driveway and the sandstone exterior of the farmhouse peered out from beneath winding ivy and wisteria stalks. The house looked big but cosy, and Isla couldn't wait to get inside the wooden front door. The door was oval shaped and had black iron rivets up and down in rows. The lock looked very old and secure. Around the oval door was a flagstone border with little carvings of faeries and flowers edged into the stone, Isla gasped at the intricate detail of the carvings. To the right of the front door, which was nestled in the centre of the farmhouse, bloomed a little side garden, nestled behind trestles of foliage. Isla could see overgrown patches if plants and imagined this was the kitchen garden which her grandad had talked about before.

Grandad Monty ambled from the car, far more confident on his feet than he had been in London, and marched up to the front door. He touched the faerie carvings gently with a careful hand, his mind elsewhere. Isla's mum came behind him, juggling her handbag and a set of keys. She jumbled the keys together, making a show of looking for the big old brass key that fit the lock in the front door. Slowly, she clicked the key left in the lock and the door fell open inwards, revealing the hallway of the house. The weather had turned grey again and Isla fell a chill in the fresh afternoon air; she was eager to get inside.

The hallway was dusty and had a mouldy scent, like a cupboard that hadn't been opened for a very long time. Through the hallway, Isla could see the living room, which had big leather sofas and chairs. The room looked cosy and there were bookshelves on every available wall, brimming with books. At the back of the living room, flooding the space with light, were a set of enormous windows that looked out onto a rolling field, which cascaded across the landscape as far as the eye could see. The entrance hall was circular with an antique dresser in the middle, balancing a vase with dead, dried flowers. Isla's mum grabbed the flowers and swished through another door, revealing a huge kitchen.

Inside the kitchen was a gigantic oak table to the left, flanked by benches and cushions big enough for ten people at least. To the right, housed in a giant inglenook fireplace, stood an old stove, which Grandad Monty had told Isla was left on all year round. A terrific warmth filled the air and the room felt cosy in the autumn chill. Through the window of the kitchen, Isla could see the overgrown garden, with relics of vegetable patches and herb gardens strewn about. This was to be Grandad Monty's project and contribution to the household; he would transform the garden back to its former glory, growing everything himself, and make enough vegetable pie to feed the whole village.

Isla walked through the warm kitchen as her mum switched on the glowing lights, illuminating the space and revealing its size. The ceilings were vast and high, with pots and pans hanging from a giant rack in the middle of the room. Beneath the rack was a gigantic chopping board, which sat upon a large wooden structure filled with drawers for storing cutlery and knives. At the other end of the kitchen was a stable door, and Isla slid the bolt, pushing it open. Outside was a path: if you turned right, you would find yourself in the kitchen garden; if you went left, the path led you around the back of the house. Isla ventured to the left, her heart pounding with excitement. She had never had this much space in London; everything felt so vast and overwhelming.

The field at the back of the house continued as far as her eyes could see. Just outside the room where the big sofas were lay some garden furniture, tilted on its side to guard it from the weather. Isla tipped the chairs back upright and slumped down into one of them, leaving the table face down as it was too heavy. In the grass next to the garden furniture, Isla noticed a little pit which had been dug into the ground – for a fire, perhaps? She grinned at the prospect of sitting around a fire as her grandad told stories, toasting marshmallows and cuddling under blankets.

"Isla!" came a voice from inside the house.

Isla skipped back around to the kitchen and poked her head in through the stable door, which had swung half open.

"Neigh!" remarked Isla playfully, tipping her head up and down like a horse.

Her mum was inside the kitchen, already putting her cookbooks onto the shelves. "Darling, the removal lorry is here. They were a lot quicker than I thought they would be. I don't want Grandad to lift a finger so perhaps you could take him for a walk for me? I know he will try to help if he's here, stubborn old man." She rolled her eyes upwards and put her hands on her hips defiantly.

"Sure Mum, I would love to. We can walk down to the village, or maybe even the beach!" exclaimed Isla.

"Yes, the village is just a short walk down the driveway, but please make sure Grandad has his hat on... and you! Your wellington boots are in the hallway, I packed them in the car because I knew the mud would be terrible. Grandad needs his stick as well; Isla, please don't let him tell you he can walk without it. The gravel and the mud make him unsteady on his feet..." Isla's mum trailed off, searching in her handbag. Eventually, she pulled out her wallet and withdrew a £20 note from inside. "Here sweetie, just in case." She pushed the money into Isla's coat pocket and continued arranging her cookbooks onto big wooden shelves lining the walls of the kitchen.

Isla returned to the hallway and found her grandad quietly looking at an old black and white photograph in a wooden frame on the wall. The frame was once again carved with faeries and mermaids. Isla approached him cautiously.

"What's that, Grandad?" she asked.

Grandad Monty started a little before he realised it was Isla standing next to him. "Oh, Isla, this is your Grandma Ivy, see here... this is her, this is me, and this is your mum when she was just a little dot. Always up to no good that girl, had a head full of clouds, just like someone else I know. She were always playing outside and never coming when she was called for supper. She got that from your grandma." Grandad Monty smiled, staring out of the living room windows.

"Grandad, let's go for a walk. I want to see the village and Mum's unpacking..."

Isla winced as she gave the game away.

"We can't go for a walk, Isla, we have to help your mum. Can't be skiving off now when there's work to be done, pet. Back in my day I could lift three boxes all at once! Let's see if I can still beat my record..." Grandad Monty stumbled off in the direction of the removal lorry. "Gotta show these young fellas a thing or two..."

Isla raced to catch up and blocked his path immediately. Monty looked down at his granddaughter, who stared up at him pleadingly.

"Oh, for heaven's sake," he grunted. "All right... you win. You and your silly mother. I won't die from carrying a box, you know?"

Isla smiled sheepishly back at him.

"Get my stick, old pal, and I'll show you around..."

CHAPTER 8

ST SENARA'S SECRET

Grandad Monty and Isla walked out of the open front door as the removal men shifted the boxes along a chain of arms and legs, with Isla's mum guiding them from the front.

Grandad Monty looked back at the scene with a raised eyebrow as his daughter bossed the men around with tenacity. "Seems your mum has it all sorted anyway."

They ambled slowly down the path, soaking in the fresh air and listening to the birds calling from the hedgerows on either side of the driveway. At the end of the path, they crossed the little burbling brook, which trickled fresh water down past the village. Blackberries bulged from brambles and Isla picked a couple to eat. The delicious berries burst tart flavour into her mouth and stained her tongue a vibrant shade of fuchsia.

After crossing the small brook, the pair found themselves in the heart of the village. Before them towered the ancient church. At the beginning of the pathway up to the church door stood a stone sign with the name 'St Senara's Parish'.

Isla tugged at her grandad's sleeve. "Look, Grandad! From the story! The one about the mermaid's chair – from Tales of Zennor."

Grandad Monty smiled and tapped his nose mischievously. "Let's go inside, shall we?"

He pushed open the heavy wooden

door and revealed the interior of the building. The aisle of the church ran to an alter at the end and a lectern with a shiny, brass eagle. Along the walls were lanterns, unlit but housing well-melted candles. Wooden pews ran alongside the aisles on either side all the way to the front of the church. In the window at the end of the aisle were tiny panes of coloured glass, making the afternoon light dance about in swirls of red, green, yellow, purple, turquoise, pink and every other colour you could imagine. The church was empty and quiet; the stones made it feel cold and damp.

Isla stepped tentatively inside. To her right was a wooden bench that was different to the other pews in the church. The bench was shorter and somewhat taller, set aside from the others. She walked up to the mysterious bench and discovered an intricate carving on the right hand side. It was a mermaid, holding a brush and a shell. Isla gasped; she couldn't believe that she was seeing the bench from the story.

Grandad Monty approached from behind her. "Ah! The Mermaid's Chair! She's a beauty, isn't she? Must've taken hours to carve something like that." He stroked the smooth wood on the mermaid's long hair. "Come on, pal. Let's go and look around. I used to know the priest here but it seems he may not be in." Grandad Monty hobbled up the aisle calling, "Hello, Bernie? You in?"

His voice created a resounding echo as it bounced off the chasms of wood above their heads. Isla felt in her pocket for her miniature mermaid. She placed the tiny creature onto the chair and smiled. *Now you are home*, she thought.

"Isla!" came her grandad's voice, echoing through the church.

Isla looked up and ran towards Grandad Monty's voice, leaving the mermaid on the chair. Unbeknownst to Isla, just as she had turned her back to the chair and was halfway up the aisle, the mermaid began to glow a shade of turquoise, then the deepest emerald blue, illuminating the carving of the mermaid on the side of the chair.

Isla found her grandad inside a small room at the top of the church, hidden behind a giant tapestry of a stormy ocean.

"Look what I found, Isla." Grandad Monty held a book in his hand, looking like a naughty schoolboy who had crept into the headteacher's office.

"Grandad," whispered Isla, trying to conceal their presence, "you can't be in here... it says 'private' on the door!" Isla stood at the threshold, gesturing for her grandad to come out from behind the tapestry.

The whole building seemed to hold its breath for the two visitors inside, like it was waiting for them to leave before it could resume its slumber.

"Isla, if you go through life taking note of every single sign you see, you won't have a lot of fun," said Grandad Monty in a sing-song voice.

Isla rolled her eyes.

"Aha! You *are* your mother's daughter," said Grandad Monty, suddenly much louder, pointing at Isla and making her giggle.

Finally, she crept inside, looking left and right as if for a hidden trap. Grandad Monty held out the book as bait and Isla grabbed it as soon as she was in touching distance, still looking around. Isla liked to play by the rules – she felt like she fit into the world a lot better when she did – but she had to admit that it was fun to be a bit naughty sometimes.

She looked at the front cover of the book, which showed a mermaid with her hands raised in the air, the waves raging around her. It looked like she was commanding the ocean! The book was small enough to fit into Isla's hand and felt warm in her palm. It was clearly very old, and the pages were worn and dogeared.

"Let's borrow this for a few days," said Grandad Monty, taking the book from Isla and slipping it into his pocket. He pulled out a tiny shell from his pocket and left it where the book had previously been sat. "Don't worry," he said, noticing Isla's concerned expression. "The priest, old Bernie, will know it's me who's taken it. I used to take this book a lot as a kid. Come to think of it, me and old Bernie were both kids then; it was his grandfather who was priest at that time." Grandad Monty scratched his head, lost in a memory.

Isla tugged at his jacket. "Are you sure, Grandad?"

Grandad Monty bent down, so that he was eye level with his granddaughter. "Trust me, he will know I have the book, Isla. It's sort of an unwritten code around here." He chucked, pointing at the shell, before suddenly clamping his hand over his mouth. "But you make it seem like quite a forbidden adventure, my girl! Hush now, we mustn't get caught... let's go!" he grinned, speeding off as a fast as he could, which was not very fast at all.

Isla followed, smiling after him. He always did have a silly sense of humour.

On the way out of the old church, Isla collected the miniature mermaid from the chair, absentmindedly placing her back into her pocket.

CHAPTER 9

THE MILLER'S ARMS

Once outside the church, the autumn chill became a little fiercer. Isla pulled her jacket tight around her chest to stop herself from shivering, but Grandad Monty left his jacket open as always, hobbling off across the green with his walking stick. Isla could see a crooked old building on the other side of the green, made from grey wonky stones with whirling smoke billowing from both of its crooked chimneys. *What a curious building,* thought Isla. The windows of the old building were very low to the ground and had flower boxes attached to them, which held the last of the summer blooms.

Grandad Monty stopped midway across the green and pointed to the intriguing building. "Looks like the fires are lit, Isla," he whispered.

Above the door, a creaky old wooden sign swung in the breeze, decorated with a painting of a watermill and embossed with the words 'The Miller's Arms'.

"Come on, Isla. Let's stop by this port in a storm, my girl. That's the local pub, The Miller's Arms," he announced with pride.

Isla, although used to her grandad's unusual turns of phrase, looked confused.

Her grandad laughed heartily. "That means let's get a drink and go sit by the warm fire."

With that he marched onwards across the green in the direction of the peculiarly lopsided pub. The afternoon was starting to give way to the evening, and the sky grew darker, making the soft lights in the village more visible. Isla could see the long shadows of the cottages growing upon the green.

When they arrived at the old pub, both Isla and Grandad Monty had to duck beneath the doorframe, which had tilted with age over the many years it had stood, welcoming visitors and wanderers into the warmth of the cosy room beyond. The door jangled a small bell, which chimed loudly as the door returned to its frame. Inside the pub, the atmosphere felt warm and inviting. Soft lights glowed from the corners, where low tables occupied the spaces in the alcoves, and heavy beams snaked across the ceiling close to their heads. Next to the many fireplaces, people enjoyed hot chocolate and warm ginger beer.

Grandad Monty tapped his stick on one of the low beams above. "That's the wood from the old wreck of the *Mary Celeste*, terrible night it was meant to be! Stormy and freezin' cold. The old ship sank claiming fifty souls; left plenty of widows did that nasty storm... before I was born, mind you. This pub's been here for centuries."

The low hum of voices mixed with the smell of burning wood and the clinking of glasses comforted and relaxed Isla. As she looked around, she noticed dried flowers hanging from the roof, and a vast variety of sea shells decorating the front of the bar. Isla gasped in delight at the different patterns the shells seemed to make in the candlelight.

Suddenly, from somewhere below the bar, a woman with bright-red, tightly curled hair and a round, flushed but friendly face appeared. She stumbled up from what seemed to be a hole in the floor behind the bar, balancing a box of crisps in one hand and a bottle of juice in the other, making quite a racket in the small space. She made a sound of frustration as she tripped slightly on a very long patchwork skirt, which billowed out from her waist.

"I'm gettin' far too old to be doin' this!" she muttered in a thick Cornish accent, pulling the skirt back around her ample stomach. "Have you ever seen the likes of this before? A cellar, right in the way, right where a girl might fall and hurt herself?"

Grandad Monty and Isla stared wide-eyed at the bumbling woman, but she didn't notice them. Grandad Monty gave a loud coughing noise to get the woman's attention and she quickly turned around, clamping her wide, suspicious eyes on Grandad Monty.

"Monty?" she gasped, clamping her plump hands over her mouth.

"Betty!" boomed Grandad Monty in a

startlingly loud voice.

Other customers seated at the low tables turned to look, their eyes glinting with surprise in the candlelight.

"Monty, is it... is it really you? After all these years?" asked Betty.

"Yes, old girl! In the flesh. At your service..." He took an awkward bow, lifting is hat theatrically from his head and sweeping it in front of him while stepping back slightly from the bar.

Isla had to steady him with her arm.

The woman giggled and clapped with delight. "I can't believe it, so I can't! Let me look at you." Betty grabbed Grandad Monty's chin and pulled it forward into the light of the bar, then turned his head left and right, twice in both directions, while carefully surveying his face. "The years 'ave been good to you, Monty, unlike this old crow." She rolled her eyes upwards quickly and chuckled, letting go of

Grandad Monty's face and beaming at him.

"Nonsense!" boomed Grandad Monty. "You've not aged a day, my girl!" He winked playfully at Betty, who giggled heartily once more, then glanced down at Isla inquisitively.

"Who do we have 'ere then? She yours, Monty?"

"This is my granddaughter, Isla. My best pal, so she is," beamed Monty, tapping Isla on the head. "Imogen's girl."

"Oh, Monty, she is the spitting' image of your Ivy. Imogen's girl, well I never. Little Imogen was just a girl herself not so long ago," Betty cooed as she surveyed Isla.

"Pleased to meet you, Betty," said Isla, in her most polite meeting-new-adults tone.

"Oh, I say, what lovely manners, my girl. Manners will take you far in life, so they will," said Betty.

"Me and Isla are back in town for good, Betty. Imogen finally decided to leave London, so here we are." Grandad Monty put an arm around Isla, who smiled up at him.

"Well, this is exciting news! Our Monty, back in old Zennor. Drinks all round, I say. Well, maybe just for us three," Betty whispered, winking at Isla. "Here you are, loves. Hot ginger beer on the house."

Betty turned around and ladled two mugs full of steaming hot ginger beer with a spicy, delicious aroma. Isla breathed in the tantalising scent, reminding her of her grandad's market stall in the winter months, when he would make her hot ginger beer and tell her stories while they waited for more customers to arrive.

"Ah, thanks, old girl. It's great being back in me old village, I feel fifteen again," laughed Grandad Monty, leaning back on his walking stick. "Still making those delicious Cornish pasties, are ya?"

Betty nodded proudly in response, and Isla suddenly noticed the smell of baked pastry float into the bar.

"Aye, Barry's just cooked up another batch." Betty waved towards a door at the end of the bar.

"Isla, why don't you be a good pal and bring them drinks over there. We can sit by the fire." Grandad Monty pointed to a low table next to a smouldering fire at the far side of the bar.

Isla did as he asked and carefully carried the drinks over, placing them down gently on the wonky wooden table. Grandad Monty sighed heavily as he sunk into the worn armchair next to the crackling fire. After arranging his walking stick for easy access later, he picked up his mug and took a deep gulp of the warming liquid inside.

"Ahh," he sighed contentedly, his lips

curling from corner to corner.

Isla took a sip and gave an identical sigh, smiling from ear to ear.

Grandad Monty boomed with laughter. "Chip off the old block, aren't ya?"

From behind the bar, Betty toddled over, her skirts nestled around her. In her hand, she carried a rustic looking plate, loaded with two warm, delicious-looking Cornish pasties. Isla grinned at the sight.

"Here you go, my loves. Hot out of the oven and on the house." Betty plonked the plate down on the table with a hearty smile.

"Oh Betty, you do know the way to a man's heart," said Grandad Monty, giving her one of his winks again.

Betty laughed and toddled back over to the bar, when a loud crash came from the kitchen. Isla heard Betty shouting as she disappeared inside:

"Barry, you old goat! What are you doin' to my kitchen!"

Grandad Monty and Isla looked at each other and shrugged, before digging in to their pasties. They were absolutely delicious, and when Betty re-appeared from the kitchen, Isla asked her for the recipe.

"Of course, my girl, I'll just go write it down for ya."

A few moments later, Betty returned.

"Here you are, loves. Betty's own Cornish pasty recipe."

Ingredients

For the pastry (or you can use shop bought pastry if you like):

- 125g of chilled and diced butter
- 125g lard
- 500g plain flour
- 6 tbsp of cold water
- 1 egg, beaten

For the filling (if you don't like meat, you can use pumpkin instead):

- 350g of beef skirt, finely diced, or half a medium pumpkin, finely diced
- 1 large onion, finely chopped
- 2 medium potatoes, peeled and thinly sliced
- 175g swede, peeled and finely chopped
- 1 tsp salt
- A sprinkle of freshly ground pepper
- Betty's secret ingredient: 1/2 tsp nutmeg

Method

Step 1: Rub the butter and lard into the flour with your fingertips, then add the water to make a firm dough. Cut into four pieces, then chill for 20 minutes.

Step 2: Heat oven to 220C/fan 200C/gas 7. Mix together the filling ingredients (beef or pumpkin, potatoes, swede, onion, salt, pepper and nutmeg) then roll out each piece of dough on a lightly floured surface into a round circle (about 23cm wide). Use a plate to help you.

Step 3: Place ¼ of the filling in the centre of the pastry circle and pack it tightly. Brush some of the beaten egg all the way around the edge of the pastry circle. Carefully fold the circle over, creating a half-moon shape, and crimp the pastry together around the edges, sealing in the filling. Brush the top with the beaten egg and place on a non-stick baking tray or on baking paper.

Step 4: Bake for 10 minutes, then lower the oven temperature to 180C/fan 160C/gas 4 and cook for 45 minutes more until golden. Serve immediately to your hungry friends and family!

"Thank you, Betty! This is great," said Isla.

"Aye, thanks, Betty. We'll be sure to try it out once we've unpacked all those boxes," said Grandad Monty.

Betty gave them both a warm smile and went back to the bar, while Isla and Grandad Monty finished their pasties and ginger beer.

After a while, Grandad Monty retrieved the book from his pocket that he had borrowed from the church and laid it out on the table for Isla to look at.

Inside the book was another version of *The Mermaid of Zennor* story, but the pictures in this version showed a very tiny mermaid, although the tale was almost identical to the one she had heard back in London. The book was very old, and all of the pictures were hand drawn and painted by an artist. Isla ran her fingers over the intricate pictures and bounced in her seat with excitement about her adventure so far.

"It is said that Morveren of Zennor created many mermaid colonies around these parts... of course it's just a folk tale, but a mightily beautiful tale at that," whispered Grandad Monty over his ginger beer.

Isla ran her fingers over the gilded pages, letting the images rest in her imagination.

"Come on, Isla. We best get back before it gets too dark."

Grandad Monty tried to lift himself out of the chair using his stick, but couldn't manage it, so Isla rushed to support him. Even if her grandad didn't think he needed help, Isla would always be there just in case he did.

When they arrived back at the farmhouse, Isla's mum had already unpacked a lot of the boxes and looked very tired indeed. They removed their coats, and all gathered by the stove. Isla kept her chunky jumper on and fluffy slippers, which her mum had fished from a box of her things, to make sure she stayed extra warm below the high ceilings. Before leaving The Miller's Arms, Betty had insisted that Grandad Monty take Cornish pasties home for the family to enjoy on their first night, as nobody had thought of dinner.

Isla's mum laid out the warm Cornish pasties along with hot cups of milky tea, and everybody tucked in to the tasty filling and flaky pastry. They all devoured their delicious meal very quickly, surprisingly hungry after such a long day full of new experiences and adventures. After dinner, Grandad Monty yawned widely and declared himself off to bed. Isla's mum helped him up the stairs to his room, which was still crammed full of boxes, while Isla brushed her teeth.

"We can sort all this out, Dad, don't worry. You need to take it easy you know; a bit of rest never hurt anybody," Isla's mum said from inside Grandad Monty's room.

After she had said goodnight to Grandad Monty, Isla's mum put Isla to bed in her big, new bedroom, and she quickly drifted off to sleep, full of hope and excitement for her new life in Cornwall.

CHAPTER 10

PORTHZENNOR COVE

When Isla awoke, she could hear seagulls calling out in the distance. They were not like the ones in London; they sounded as if they were shrieking for joy – soaring and having fun in the skies – rather than begging for scraps of food like the seagulls in the city. The sun splashed her room with liquid gold tones as it shone brightly through the window, and Isla blinked her sleepy eyes twice as she adjusted to the brightness of the morning. *What time is it?* she wondered, feeling a little disorientated.

During the night, Isla had dreamt of the mermaid from St Senara's church, and she had imagined herself swimming through the waves deep into the middle of the ocean, just like a mermaid. Isla pushed the duvet from her legs, freeing her body and inviting in the cold morning. She shivered slightly and pulled a soft, knitted blanket around her from the bottom of her bed.

Tentatively, tapping her feet on the wooden floorboards, Isla approached the window and twisted the lock. With one swoosh she flung the window up and breathed the sea air deeply into her lungs. With a huge smile she surveyed the world around her; the luscious green field below basked gloriously in the morning sun, and she could just about see the waves crashing against the cliffs. Slowly, she moved from the window, pulled on her fluffy slippers and raced down the big staircase.

"Mum!" she called, as she raced into the kitchen and promptly collided with her mum, who was carrying a basket full of washing.

"Ouch!" yelled Isla's mum, holding her stomach and looking shocked, until she realised it was just Isla, who had fallen back on the floor and was now holding the side of her head, looking embarrassed. "Isla! You gave me such a fright; you need to be more careful," she gasped, winded by the collision.

"Sorry, Mum. I'm just really excited to go outside..."

Isla's mum helped her up off the floor with a proffered hand. "Why don't you go down to the beach for an hour and explore? Grandad and I need to do some boring things around the house this morning. Unpacking takes a very long time—"

Isla and her mum both looked up sharply as they heard a crash from the direction of the living room. It sounded like a mountain of books falling onto the floorboards.

"He's at it again!" complained Isla's mum. "Trying to lift things when he knows that he shouldn't. I don't know how many times I need to tell that man, he won't listen..." Her voice trailed off and she looked down at Isla. "Just go and get some fresh air, sweetheart. There is quite a lot to do, and I need to unpack your grandad's things before he does. It's amazing how much stuff you can accumulate over the years!" She patted Isla on the shoulder and quickly moved past her in the direction of the crash, leaving the washing in a heap on the floor.

"But how do I get to the beach, Mum?"

Isla asked softly, not wanting to disturb her mum when she was clearly very busy.

"Of course, I forgot you wouldn't know. Sorry, Isla. Walk over the field and down the path along the cliff, you can't miss it. I used to go when I was your age; I'd play on that beach for hours. Have fun, sweetie!" she called brightly as she left the room.

Isla was excited to go and play on the beach, but the world suddenly felt very big indeed now that she was expected to explore all by herself, especially as it was all new to her. In London, Isla knew all the streets, and there were always people around if you got lost. There were no pavements or street signs or underground trains here, and Isla had barely seen any people either. Isla took her jacket from the peg by the backdoor and shoved her hand in the pocket. She still had the money her mum had given her yesterday, and there in the other pocket was her miniature mermaid. Isla decided that she would take the mermaid to the beach and play with her in the sand, pretending she was the real Mermaid of Zennor.

Isla walked out the back door, turned left and skipped down to the end of the field, the dewy grass surrendering under her feet. The ground was starting to turn a little gooey beneath her, but she never minded a bit of mud. All she could hear were the birds singing in the hedgerows and the heavy waves crashing in the distance, which made a nice change from car horns and the noise of people talking that she heard in London.

She climbed clumsily over the wooden stile at the edge of the field, and discovered a small wildflower meadow on the other side. The meadow was wild and untamed, and was filled with beautiful, colourful flowers, sprouting up in random patterns all over the ground. Isla believed that if she were to find faeries anywhere, this is where they would live. She made a mental note to return here with a notepad and go faerie spotting.

The meadow eventually gave way to a tiny woodland in the far corner, but Isla kept on a small path which led through the flowers and down to another wooden stile. The scent of the meadow was over-powering and Isla felt heady and full of wonder. She carefully climbed over the stile and realised she was on a small path with a steep cliff in front of her. The cliff edge was far enough away that it wasn't a hazard for her, but she still felt a little exhilarated by the steep drop into the sea below. Isla dared not lean over the cliff, just in case she stumbled and fell, but she knew it was there all the same!

Isla walked slowly along the path, which

snaked all the way down onto the beach. At the bottom of the cliff, Isa jumped down onto a rock, which was partially hidden by lots of long grass that waved in the coastal wind. Before her lay an expanse of breathtaking beach. Isla squealed with delight, running across the sand as the wind swept along and pulled the grains of sand with it, swirling them in the air and dispersing them in all directions. In the distance, white-tipped waves were hauled and thrown relentlessly onto the sand, making an almighty crashing sound.

Isla pulled her jacket tight around her neck to stay warm as she ventured along the edge of the beach, peering into little rockpools made by the tide and jumping in puddles abandoned by the ocean. The salty air tangled her hair and she swept it back off her face, licking particles of salt with her tongue when her hair was whipped into her mouth by the breeze.

The day was bright but chilly, and there was no rain on the horizon, so Isla thought it was the perfect day to explore the rocks along the beach.

Eventually, she came across a powerful cascade of water falling from the cliff above, beating down on the rocks in a constant stream. Isla squinted to peer past the water flowing relentlessly from above. She could just make out what looked like the opening of a cave, hidden behind the waterfall. Isla worked up the courage, put up her hood, and ducked beneath the flowing water. A loud clatter of droplets landed on her head, almost causing her to fall into the pool of water beyond, but she managed to steady herself on a rock. Suddenly, Isla found herself behind the waterfall, looking back out through the water onto the beach.

There was a strange sense of calm about the cave, and the falling water sounded much quieter on this side. There was very little light; just enough to make out the impressive structure. Isla was standing on a rock, still attached to the beach, but below her in the centre of the cave was a deep pool of water, which continued on into the darkness of the cave further than her eyes could see. Isla wasn't sure how deep this pool of water was, but it certainly didn't look shallow. She couldn't believe her discovery! This would be the perfect place to set up her little pirate cove. *A real cove is much better than rocks in a bathtub,* she thought to herself, planning her next creation. Meanwhile, in her pocket, the miniature mermaid began to twitch...

CHAPTER 11

A TAIL OF A TIME!

Isla couldn't explore the rest of the cave without getting into the water, which she really didn't think was a good idea. She knew the water would be extremely cold, and if it was too deep, she could get stuck. Then, Isla remembered the mermaid in her pocket. Her miniature mermaid would have so much fun playing in real seawater, hidden behind the curtain of water from the beach. It was perfect!

Carefully, she lifted the tiny figure from her pocket and knelt on the rock, slowly lowering the mermaid into the deep pool below. Instantly, the entire cave lit up with twinkling lights, like tiny stars sparkling all around. Isla gasped, jumping back from the pool in surprise. In her shock, she had released the miniature mermaid. A beautiful, mesmerising singing voice suddenly arose from the pool of water and Isla leaned over in amazement to find the sound. She couldn't believe what she was seeing... the tiny mermaid had come to life right there in the water and was singing with glee, swooshing her tail and swimming in delighted circles, her hair trailing behind her like silk. Isla gasped once more and the mermaid swung around in the water with fright, covering her face with her hands as if to hide.

"Hello," whispered Isla, not wanting to scare the little creature.

The mermaid poked a tiny eye from behind her hands and eventually lowered her hands in curiosity.

119

"My name is Isla, I bought you here from London, please don't worry. I won't hurt you. What's your name?"

"My name... is Zennor," said the mermaid in a musical voice. "Where is L-on-d-on?" she stammered cocking her head at Isla as she floated in the water, feeling more at ease now that she knew Isla was a friend.

Isla grinned, she couldn't believe how her day had turned out! "London is the capital city of England, it's where I used to live until I moved here, and my grandad gave you to me. He bought you from a market in Padstow; that's not too far from here."

The mermaid looked confused, then let out a loud yelp, spinning in circles. "Padstow! Oh no, oh no... the market... it's all coming back to me now. I got caught in a fishing net. I was outside of the cave – mermaids should never leave their cave –

and, well I..." She trailed off, her eyes welling with tiny tears. "I must have ended up at the market because when we are out of the sea water, we turn solid, and we can't move anymore!"

"The market trader must have thought you were a statue," said Isla.

"Yes, maybe... but how did I end up back here?" asked the mermaid.

"Ah, well, you see, we just moved here yesterday. I came with my mum and my grandad. I was exploring the beach and then I found this cave. I wanted to see how you would look in the water and, well... here we are!"

The mermaid continued to stare with wide, glittering eyes. "You saved me!" she said, a massive grin on her miniature face. "How could I ever repay you, Isla?"

"Oh no, it's my pleasure! I am so happy you are safe and home at last. Who'd have thought I was carrying around a real mermaid in my pocket. Are there more mermaids like you here?" asked Isla.

"Oh yes!" said Zennor. "There are hundreds of mermaids just like me... in fact... I know how I can repay you, Isla!" Zennor started spinning once more in excited circles, a little jingling laugh arising from her lips. "I have magical powers you see."

Isla looked confused, so Zennor continued.

"This is my mother's cove, and she has missed me dearly, I am sure. I would love for you to meet her, so she may thank you herself and offer you a gift. It is custom here in the cove."

"Oh! That would be wonderful," exclaimed Isla. "Can you bring her to me?"

"I am going to do better than that. I am going to bring you to her!" replied Zennor, giggling.

Isla was even more confused. The cave,

although now twinkling with many lights, seemed dark and dangerous, and she wasn't very good at swimming. "I can't swim very well, Zennor, so I am a little scared to go in there." Isla pointed at the deep, cold pool of water.

"Isla, you saved my life. Now, you must trust me. All is not what it seems, I promise. Please, come into the water."

Isla was reminded of Matthew in the story her grandad had told her; of how the mermaid had coaxed him into the crashing waves... he was never seen again. What if that happened to her?

"I'm not sure, Zennor..." said Isla, shaking her head.

"Trust me," smiled the little creature.

Isla closed her eyes, breathing deeply. Then she counted slowly to ten.

Suddenly, with a splash and a small leap, Isla was in the freezing pool, her head under the water and her arms thrashing around. What had she done?

Panicking, she closed her eyes and thrashed around some more, until she realised she definitely wasn't dreaming. She needed to calm down in order to swim. Ever so slowly, Isla slowed her movements, then opened her eyes, gazing up at the twinkling surface of the water. She could see the soft lights above her. In the distance, Zennor's iridescent tail was swishing in the water.

Isla no longer felt cold or afraid. She swam with a wonderful, easy grace which she had never been able to do before. Her head broke the surface and she looked down at herself, her mouth falling open in amazement. A magnificent, orange, sparkling tail swung effortlessly in the water below her where her legs should be. It was her tail... she had a tail! Isla gasped, suddenly panicking, but Zennor grabbed her hands and held them tightly, facing her as she smiled comfortingly. Isla realised she was now the same size as the miniature mermaid!

"What's happening?" screamed Isla. "Where are my legs? Why am I so tiny?"

"I told you I had magical powers, Isla!" giggled her new friend. "I wanted you to see for yourself. Don't worry, once you leave the pool you will return to your normal state... a giant," laughed Zennor, still holding Isla's hands in her own.

Isla swished her tail violently back and forth, causing a splash on the surface of the pool. Zennor giggled again.

"Don't worry, the more you practice, the better you will be at using your tail. Practice makes perfect, so they say!"

Isla finally returned Zennor's bright smile and gave her a huge hug in thanks. "I always wanted to have a great Cornish adventure, but I never thought it would be this exciting!" said Isla.

"Well, this is going to be quite an adventure for you,' replied Zennor, grinning from ear to ear. "Now, let's go! It's time for you to meet everybody. But we must be secretive..."

With that, Zennor dove beneath the water and Isla followed, noticing that her tail pushed her effortlessly where she needed to go – she didn't even have to try.

CHAPTER 12

THE KINGDOM OF MINIATURE
MERFOLK

Isla and Zennor swam into the darkness of the cave. The world looked completely different from below the surface of the water, and Isla kept wanting to swim up to take a breath, but she soon relaxed into the notion that she didn't need to *breathe* anymore. The two miniature mermaids swam further and further, until Isla noticed more twinkling lights in the distance. As they approached, Zennor took Isla's hand, guiding her forward. Isla gasped in amazement The water in front of them was filled with miniature mermaids! Isla suspected that if she were her usual, full-sized self, this magical world beneath the water would look just like the miniature worlds she created at home, only this one was real.

Zennor winked playfully at Isla and continued swimming forward, guiding Isla towards a huge set of gates, decorated beautifully with different shells. The gates were open but guarded by seahorses, upon which sat mermen in spiky shell helmets. Mermaids and mermen drifted in and out of the gates, chatting in groups or in pairs. Everybody was smiling and seemed happy; nobody noticed Isla's presence as she mingled in the crowd. Suddenly, the intimidating gates were upon them, but Isla felt a little reluctant to go through and desperately tugged at Zennor's hand, trying to bury her anxiety.

"Zennor, is this where you live? There are so many miniature mermaids... and what about those seahorses?" Isla asked, pointing in their direction.

The seahorses wore proud, regal expressions, their heads held high and straight as they bobbed up and down in the water. The mermen on their backs sat equally as proud and straight, with tiny swords at their belts and serious expressions on their faces. Zennor looked in the direction of where Isla pointed.

"Oh, don't worry about them. They work for my mother. Besides, they are here to protect us. I know they look a bit scary, but they won't even notice us," Zennor reassured her with a smile.

Isla nodded her head in amazement, unable to look away from the beautiful seahorses as they dipped up and down regally in the current.

"Come on, you are safe here., please

don't worry. We're almost there."

The two mermaids carried on through the giant shell gates, weaving in and out of the other mermaids and mermen. Inside the gates were tiny streets made of sand, lined with more shells and little tufts of seagrass as far as Isla could see. Pink shrimps manoeuvred up and down, hoovering debris and small particles from the water. Isla's jaw dropped.

"They're the street cleaners," whispered Zennor, noticing Isla's eyes move with the motion of the shrimps.

They continued down a very wide street. On either side were little stalls, flanked by mermen and mermaids selling what looked like food. Sea grasses and seaweeds of all varieties, shapes and colours were displayed on the stalls as their occupants called out into the street:

"Come get your grasses and your weeds! These crazy prices won't last forever!"

"Buy one get one free on delicious kelp! Special discount – today only!"

Isla's head swivelled this way and that as they dodged customers and traders in the busy marketplace. Isla noticed that some of the stalls were attached to tiny seahorses, just like the ones on the gates but without their regal demeanour. These seahorses were lazily munching on seagrass as their owners worked on the stalls. Nobody seemed to notice the outsider and her continuously amazed expression as they worked their way through the busy market.

Alongside the streets were little houses made from shells. Isla could see washing hanging up in gardens, small car-like carriages which looked like coconut husks, and more of the cleaning shrimps roaming around. The mermen and mermaids were all different shapes, sizes and colours. Some had bright purple tails and turquoise hair, some had orange tails and green hair, but all of them were startlingly magical in appearance. Zennor carefully guided Isla along, patiently pulling her by the hand if she stopped for too long to stare.

"We need a small disguise," whispered Zennor, suddenly stopping at the side of the street behind a huge kelp tree.

"Why do you need a disguise?" questioned Isla.

"I'll explain later, but for now..." Zennor searched around rapidly, looking for something. "Ah! You see that shell over there? Can you fetch it for me?" Zennor was pointing towards a big conch shell, discarded in someone's front garden.

Isla nodded and swam to fetch the shell, and when she looked around, she saw a few mermaids wearing similar shells. Isla handed the shell to Zennor, who arranged it carefully on her head. The shell was a bit big so it dropped, covering her eyes a little. Isla giggled and helped Zennor rearrange the shell so that she could see. Before long, the two mermaids were howling with laughter.

"Okay, okay, let's go," giggled Zennor, once they had eventually managed to position the shell so she could still see.

The two new friends swam on.

"This is the centre of the mercity," announced Zennor as they came to a large square.

Isla noticed some slightly bigger shell buildings, which looked like they had taken a lot longer to build than the houses.

"This is the merparliament building... that's the merhospital... over there is the merlibrary... the merschool is down there…. oh, and the seahorse academy is over there!"

Zennor pointed in different directions, but Isla couldn't take it all in. The mermaid city was huge! Much bigger than she had first realised.

"And there… there is my home!" Zennor pointed finally to a sparkling, palatial building, covered with shells in all sorts of beautiful, intricate patterns in every colour of the rainbow.

Isla's jaw fell open once again. "You live there?" The building was the most beautiful structure Isla had ever seen, and went so high that it rose above the surface of the water.

"Yes, this is the palace. My mother is… sort of the queen around here…" Zennor looked a little flushed, almost like she was embarrassed.

"The queen?" exclaimed Isla, without realising how loud her voice was as the words slipped from her lips.

"Shh... Isla, please. We need to sneak inside," whispered Zennor, pulling Isla towards her.

"If you live here, why do we need to sneak in?"

"Well, it's just that... I am kind of in trouble... you see, when a mermaid goes missing, it is very serious. Nobody from the outside world is supposed to know about our cove, but... I'm just so fascinated by the humanfolk! When I went missing, I was sort of doing a project on them... er... you... well, yes, your people, I guess... and my mother told me I had to stop because it's dangerous and the humanfolk are not friendly... but I knew she was wrong, and I was right! You're lovely." Zennor rambled so quickly that Isla almost missed what she was saying.

"Wait, hold on... you mean, you need to sneak *me* in?" asked Isla with alarm.

"Er, yes, well... I suppose... yeah," replied Zennor, once again looking slightly embarrassed.

"I really don't like the sound of that, Zennor... those guards on the door look scary... what if they realise I'm not really a mermaid? What if they realise I'm one of the... *humanfolk*," asked Isla, very concerned.

"Isla, trust me, they will never know the difference. My magic is unrivalled in this cove; even my mother hasn't got a patch on me. It was a gift from our founder, the great Morveren. We are all descendants from her—"

"Wait... did you say Morveren?" Isla grasped Zennor by the shoulders. "Morveren... Morveren... that's the Mermaid of Zennor! The one from my grandad's book!" Isla gasped in surprise as everything suddenly started to fall into place.

Zennor looked confused. "Morveren is our founder; she created this cove many centuries ago. She used to be just a single mermaid by herself and she was cursed. A wicked sea sprite condemned her to roam the oceans alone unless she found the voice of a pure soul. Mermaids and sea sprites have been at war for thousands of years. Eventually, Morveren found the voice she needed to break the curse. She was swimming one day, not far from here, and heard the voice of a man, coming from a church in a village for the humanfolk. He had the most magical singing voice, and she knew right away that he would be the one to save her. Once she had found a way to walk on land and find him, she brought the man – Matthew he was called – into the ocean, and all of a sudden the evil curse lifted. That devilish sea sprite was defeated and then Morveren created my grandmother using her magic, in order to protect Porthzennor Cove. It's where my name comes from, actually. Since then, we have built up our mercity," Zennor replied proudly, spinning around, twirling Isla in the water so she could see around the square once again.

"That's why she never returned to the Mermaid's Chair... at St Senara's Church," gasped Isla. "Where is she now?"

"Oh, once we were created, she left Cornwall. She has travelled the seven seas with Matthew, creating new mermaid colonies wherever she can. Mermaids used to be in high numbers all across the seas until they were destroyed by the evil sea spirites, leaving just poor Morveren. Imagine being all along for centuries..." Zennor wiped away a tiny tear from the corner of her eye as her mind drifted to the past.

"Zennor, have any other humans ever

been here?" Isla asked urgently.

Zennor scratched her head, thinking. "Well, there was one... but nobody knows what happened to him. Apparently, one of the mermaids brought him here, but they were cast out of the colony," replied Zennor. "That's why my mother doesn't like humans... she used to keep a lot of information from me, adult stuff I guess. That's why I became so curious about the humanfolk." Zennor clamped a hand over her mouth; she had said too much.

The silence left a chasm between the two new friends, as Isla began to process all of this new information.

"Zennor, please can I go back now? I do want to come back again, really, I do, but I'm worried my mum and grandad will be missing me. You see, it was my first time visiting the beach all by myself and my mum will probably have lunch ready by now..."

Zennor smiled kindly at Isla. "Of course, Isla. It's pretty lonely in that palace – all I do all day is study, really – so I would love for you to come back! Ooh, I would love to study your people more closely, too. I want to know everything about life in the outside world. Oh, Isla, this is going to be so much fun! You can study my world and I can study your world, but in secret…"

Isla gave Zennor a huge hug. "That sounds perfect! We have so much to teach each other."

The two mermaids giggled, then Zennor clasped Isla's hand in hers and led her back through the market and outside the huge shell gates. Carefully and secretively, she took Isla back to the pool at the entrance to the cave where they had first met earlier that day. As the two mermaids surfaced in the silent pool, the twinkling lights flicked back to life again, illuminating the rocky chasm.

"I am so pleased to have met you, Isla. We'll see each other again soon," promised Zennor. "Now, on the count of three, you need to swim down below and then propel yourself as fast and as hard as you can out of the water... just like a dolphin jumping out of the ocean. That's how you return to your normal body."

Isla looked concerned. "Okaaay..." she mumbled.

"Ready?" said Zennor. "I am going to do my spell as you jump... 1... 2... 3..." counted Zennor slowly, closing her eyes and focusing very hard on her spell.

On the count of three, Isla plunged below, using the full force of her new tail to propel herself out of the water and into the air. Her stomach did a backflip, like she was on a rollercoaster, and she started to descend back towards the surface of the pool. Suddenly, with a burst of light, she landed on the side of the pool in her normal clothes, completely dry and her normal size again.

"Wow!" said Isla, clamping her hand over her mouth. She had her normal voice back again, and it was piercingly loud in the cave.

"I did it!" squealed Zennor, splashing about with delight in the pool.

"Well done, Zennor," said Isla, giving her a tiny high five with her pinky finger. "I'll see you again soon. How about tomorrow morning at nine a.m.?" she asked.

"I don't know your humanfolk time... perhaps you can teach me? I will know when you arrive in the cave – it's part of my magical powers – so when I sense that you've arrived I will swim back here." Zennor smiled, then, with a little wave goodbye, she dove beneath the waves, extinguishing the twinkling lights as she went.

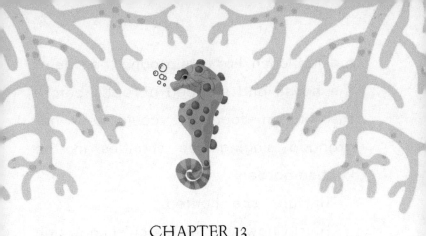

CHAPTER 13

A WHEELY RISKY RIDE

Isla ran back up the wild beach, stumbling on her legs, which felt like they belonged to someone else after using her tiny tail all morning. She couldn't believe what she had found! How had her grandad and her mum never found this magical community of mermaids?

Running back through the wild meadow, the faeries she had imagined earlier that day suddenly felt like a real possibility; she had arrived in a land of magic! As she ran back over the field, she saw her mum in the kitchen window, making lunch. Isla tore around the side of the house and stopped abruptly before the kitchen door. She could hear her grandad singing sea shanties in the kitchen garden.

"Hi Mum!" she shouted.

"Hi Isla, how was the beach? I knew you would love it," her mum said, as she sliced cheese and tomatoes for their sandwiches.

"Hello old pal!" Grandad Monty appeared in front of Isla, brandishing a trowel and wearing gardening gloves. "This place is full of weeds, but it feels great to be gardenin' again. Glad you found the beach, my girl." He clapped Isla on the shoulder and winked playfully, stumbling back to the garden, alarmingly without his stick.

Isla noticed it resting against the stone wall and ran after her grandad to help him. "Grandad! Porthzennor Cove is amazing," she exclaimed, bursting with energy.

Grandad Monty's glasses were on the end of his nose as he stopped to survey his granddaughter's face. He laughed jovially and pushed his glasses back into place, turning his attention to a tangled bed of weeds, waving the trowel like a sword.

"Ah yes, I knew you'd love it there. Wild landscape, so it is," Grandad Monty replied, before starting to hum a sea shanty.

Isla realised he was busy in his garden and didn't want to be disturbed, so she placed his stick as close to him as she could.

"You know Mum will moan if you don't have it close by," she shrugged, and Grandad Monty let out a groan of despair.

Isla skipped back to the kitchen to find her mum plating up rounds of cheese and tomato sandwiches.

"Did you have fun, darling?" her mum asked, placing the platter of sandwiches on the table where a hot pot of tea sat beside three mugs.

"Oh Mum, it's beautiful! I love it here," blurted Isla, not knowing what to do with all of the energy she suddenly had, and not wanting to reveal her secret just yet.

"I used to feel like that when I was your age." Her mum smiled, pouring milk into a jug. "Go and get your grandad for lunch, sweetie, will you?"

Isla skipped into the garden, but she couldn't see her grandad. Hurrying over to where he had been weeding, she found him face down in a pile of mud.

"Grandad!" cried Isla. "What are you doing?"

Grandad Monty lifted his torso slowly and reached for his stick, which Isla grabbed and pushed into his palm, pulling

146

him up by the elbows.

"Sorry, my girl, the old knees gave way." Grandad Monty looked slightly disorientated and wobbled on his stick.

"Our secret, mind you. Your mum won't let me come out here if she thinks my knees are that bad." Grandad Monty looked concerned.

"Please be careful, Grandad," begged Isla, holding him tight on his elbow and walking him inside.

"Oh, don't you worry, plenty of life left in these legs." Grandad Monty knocked his knees together, making her giggle.

Isla followed her grandad inside, watching for any faltering in his steps so that she could grab him, but he seemed to be just fine.

"Oh, a lovely cup of tea! Thanks, my girl," Grandad Monty said as he creakily placed himself on the end of the bench at the table.

Isla's mum smiled and gave him a pat on the shoulder. "Right you two, I'm off to do some work, okay? You both be good!"

Isla's mum poured out the hot tea into the mugs and winked at Grandad Monty, who retorted with a shrug. She left the room balancing a cup of tea on top of a notebook, a piece of sandwich half in her mouth, secured by her front teeth.

"Looks like it's just us, old pal," smiled Grandad Monty.

Hungrily, they tucked into their sandwiches and Grandad Monty told Isla his grand plans for the kitchen garden. He went into great detail about what he was going to plant and when so that they would have delicious veggies, herbs and fruit all year round. Isla smiled and listened, but her mind was back in the magical cove. After some time, once her grandad had finished, Isla tentatively asked him if he remembered anything about the beach from when he was a lad.

"Well, I haven't been for quite some years, and when I were a young lad, I found it wild down there, full of magic, if you get my drift? Come to think of it, it'd be nice to go down to the beach again soon. Maybe you can help me?"

Isla nodded slowly, a small grin beginning in the corners of her mouth.

After lunch, a sleepy silence descended on the kitchen and Grandad Monty began to close his eyes, a shaft of sunlight warming his face. Isla was busy formulating her plan to get her grandad down to the beach without any injuries, when she suddenly had a rather marvellous idea.

Around the back of the house, Isla crept through the overgrown brambles to find a small shed. The wooden ensemble was rustic and smelled of damp wood, mixed with wet grass. Isla batted away the last of the brambles and blew the cobwebs from the lock. Fortunately, the lock had been left open and the door could be pulled. With an almighty tug, the door flew agape on its creaky hinges a lot faster than Isla was expecting, cracking against its enthusiastic intruder. Isla fell back into the brambles with a yelp!

From her position tangled within the brambles, Isla scrabbled to her feet and tentatively entered the old shed. At the back, in perfect view, was a large green (and slightly rusted) wheelbarrow. Isla strode over, checking for spiders as she went, and tugged the handles upwards. The tyre was still inflated and the wheelbarrow seemed to be in working order. Carefully, Isla backed out of the shed, grabbing a large spade on her way to use as a bramble basher. Off she went, dragging the wheelbarrow and clearing her path back to the house. Isla was delighted with her prize. Luckily, nobody had heard her mission, and the house remained silent.

Leaving the wheelbarrow beneath the window, she skipped back into the sleepy kitchen through the side door, left open in her haste. Isla suddenly worried that her grandad would be cold, but there he was, slumped back in his bench seat, eyes closed with his stick fallen on the floor. Isla could hear loud snores cascading from his nose.

"Grandad," whispered Isla, going right up to his left ear as he snoozed, trying to be as quiet as possible so as not to scare him.

Nothing happened.

"Grandad," repeated Isla, this time a lot louder.

Grandad Monty awoke with a flurry of arms. "Yes, Sergeant Major!" he shouted into the air as he jumped from sleep.

Isla looked at him with a startled expression and Grandad Monty looked back at her blearily, like a small child who had been woken from a long afternoon nap.

"Isla, old pal, you scared me half to death! I were dreamin' bout the war; thought you were the Sergeant Major wakin' me up!"

Isla couldn't stifle her giggle and the pair snorted with laughter as Grandad Monty did a little comic salute to attention.

"Grandad, I have a plan to get you to the beach," Isla gasped through her giggles.

"I likes a plan, I do, my girl," Grandad Monty replied, rubbing his hands together.

"Quick! Follow me before Mum finds out. We must be quiet."

Grandad Monty nodded and Isla helped

him up from the bench, replacing his stick firmly in his hand and ushering him out into the garden. Isla revealed the wheelbarrow with a 'ta dah!' and Grandad Monty started to laugh, quickly stopping himself as he recalled their pact of silence. Instead, a wicked smile tickled the corners of his mouth.

"Right old mate, let's have at ya," he whispered, tapping the wheelbarrow with his stick. "I suppose you want me in there?"

Isla had placed all of the cushions from the outside furniture into the wheelbarrow, so that it looked more like a throne for a king rather than a gardener's tool. Without warning, Grandad Monty flopped backward into the wheelbarrow and the thing rocked side to side. He swayed with the to-and-fro without a care in the world, but Isla squeaked in panic, thinking she had made a terrible mistake.

That is, until she saw Grandad Monty lying peacefully with his legs dangling either side, waving his stick in the air.

"Didn't expect that from your old Grandad Monty, did ya?" he boomed, very pleased with himself.

"Shh Grandad! Mum will go mad if she sees... this." Isla waved her hand at the bizarre scene in front of her.

"What she don't know, don't hurt," insisted Grandad Monty.

Isla shrugged and hurriedly lifted the handles on the wheelbarrow. The thing was surprisingly light and Grandad Monty looked rather comfortable on his cushions, so Isla started off down the little path along the field towards the beach, the wheelbarrow swaying slightly but moving successfully in the right direction.

Grandad Monty chuckled with delight all the way down, using his stick as a navigation tool and waving it ahead of the wheelbarrow, pointing out rogue stones and tree roots. Isla began to work up quite a sweat with the whole ordeal, but enjoyed seeing her grandad so happy. Along the way, Grandad Monty gave a verbal tour of the different memories he had of various places they passed by, until the two of them reached the top of the very steep, winding path down to the beach.

"Ah," sighed Isla. "I forgot about this part."

Grandad Monty turned, tapping her on the shoulder with his stick. "You got me this far, a bit more won't hurt. Don't worry, pal. It'll be fine. Just tip me out if it gets bad!"

Grandad Monty winked and Isla knew that the desire to get back to his old beach was far more important to him than his safety. Isla nodded with some hesitation and resumed her position at the handlebars of the wheelbarrow. The path was actually quite manageable as long as you didn't look down over the cliff too often. Grandad Monty stayed very still in his wheelbarrow until they reached the edge of the beach, and Isla let out a sigh of relief. The sand wouldn't let the wheelbarrow pass any longer, but Isla noticed a little stump of wood which marked the path.

"Grandad, I'm going to tip the wheelbarrow up and as I do you push on your stick and then steady yourself against that tree stump. Okay?"

Grandad Monty looked nervous, then remembered he would otherwise be stuck in the wheelbarrow. "You'll tip me out like old potatoes, will ya? Quite the engineer, aren't you, Isla. Right, I'm ready."

"Okay, on the count of three..."

With every count, Isla swung the wheelbarrow upwards a little higher, and on the count of three she pushed upwards with all of her might. Terror suddenly hit her as she lowered the wheelbarrow back down, narrowly missing her feet. Miraculously, Grandad Monty was upright, balancing on his stick and the tree stump. *Phew!*

CHAPTER 14

GRANDAD'S GRAND ADVENTURE!

After some effort, the pair eventually reached the entrance to the cove, and Isla was already prepared – she had brought a backpack with an umbrella, note paper and something else…

"Okay Grandad," Isla called over the crashing of the water. "In we go!"

With a whoosh, the umbrella sprang to life, creating an effective barrier between the two of them and the cascading, cold water. Isla nodded her head at Grandad Monty as she walked below the waterfall; the sound of the flow hitting the cloth canopy created quite a racket, and Grandad Monty had to shout a little to be heard.

"Why on Earth are we goin' in here, Isla?"

"Just trust me!" Isla replied.

Grandad Monty closed his eyes and Isla panicked, lurching forward to grab his arm.

"Grandad? Are you okay?"

Grandad Monty opened one eye suspiciously. "Oh, you're still here, I thought I might be dreamin'." He waited for a response with a raised eyebrow. Then, realising his joke had gone completed over Isla's head, he rolled his eyes. "Okay, I trust you, old pal. Give an old fool a hand, will ya?"

Isla steadied Grandad Monty on her arm, holding the umbrella aloft with the other, and before long they were inside the murky cave. Water droplets dripped heavily from the roof into the pool of water below, creating a continuous echoing noise all around them. Before Isla could explain, thousands of twinkling lights began to ignite from all the hidden crevices of the cave, just like the first time.

Grandad Monty looked horrified, as if he were preparing for an ambush, moving his head rapidly in all different directions as the cave grew brighter and brighter.

"What the Dickens..." he blurted, noticing Isla's excitement.

Before she could answer, Zennor appeared in the pool of icy water, clapping her hands in delight.

"You came back!" the tiny mermaid squealed, flipping about in the water, making miniature ripples with her sparkling tail. Suddenly, Zennor noticed Grandad Monty, and darted beneath the surface.

"Zennor, come back! It's okay, he's my

grandad. He's family, we can trust him."
Isla pulled up Grandad Monty's arm and
waved it for him in the direction of the
pool.

Grandad Monty stood motionless, his
mouth so wide open that he could be
mistaken for a fly trap as he stared into
the water where Zennor had been,
unblinking.

Zennor popped her teeny forehead
above the water, leaving her hair
covering most of her face, except for one
glinting, suspicious eye. She watched Isla
waving Grandad Monty's arm and
eventually began to move her hair from
her face.

"Are you sure we can trust the old man?
He has curious humanfolk customs."
Zennor watched Grandad Monty's waving
hand curiously, trying to copy his
movements.

Isla laughed, reassuring Zennor that he

was someone who could keep their secret sacred. Grandad Monty eventually started blinking, opening then closing his mouth and making funny sucking noises.

"Can he speak the language of the humanfolk?" questioned Zennor, cocking her head to the left and watching Grandad Monty with some fascination and amusement, mimicking his smacking noises with her mouth.

"Oh yes, of course he can. Grandad!" shouted Isla loudly.

All of a sudden, Grandad Monty awoke from his shock and stammered words at Zennor. "You... you are... a real... a real mermaid. But... you were a statue... I bought you from that old crone in Padstow... you're the figurine I gave to Isla..." Grandad Monty started bouncing on his good leg, using his walking stick to balance on the other. "All these years I searched for your kind, every day. I never

ever gave up hope that you'd be real, and then I bought that tiny model in Padstow... Isla... is that? It can't be, surely..."

Isla beamed, nodding her head. "Yep! That model was Zennor the whole time, Grandad. I brought her here, set her free in the pool and now here she is."

"Wait!" squeaked Zennor. "You rescued me in Padstow? You're the one who gave me to Isla? You saved me from the ghastly fisherman!" Zennor span in a little circle in the water. "How could I ever repay you, kind sir?"

Grandad Monty looked bewildered. "The doll..." he whispered almost to himself. "She was real... she's real..."

"I know!" squealed Isla, suddenly spotting an opportunity. "Let's bring Grandad to the cove, Zennor. He knows more about Cornwall than anybody every could; he can teach you so much, just like he taught me about your people. He even

has a book about your kind... here, look..."
Isla rummaged in her backpack and
pulled out *The Book Of Zennor*.

Zennor cooed in awe at the book and
nodded her head furiously. "Yes, yes, I
want to learn, please help me learn! But
we must be careful not to rouse suspicion
in the colony... I know! We will say that you
are from The Indian Ocean Trading
Company, and you are here for business.
We get plenty of traveling traders, ever
since the turtle highway opened up last
year between here and the Seychelles.
You will need to do a couple of tasks while
you are here, but we can sort that out
later on..." Zennor trailed off as she made
plans and lists in her head.

"Isla, what is happening?" questioned
Grandad Monty.

He looked scared and a little lost. Isla
had never seen her grandad's expression
look like that before, and she worried that

she might have pushed him too far. He was getting old after all, and she had dragged him into this adventure without his permission.

"Grandad, I'm sorry for scaring you. If you don't want to go, I can just take you home in the wheelbarrow. To visit the colony, you have to jump into the water and... look I know this sounds crazy, but when you jump in, you automatically turn into a mermaid! The water is enchanted, see. But we don't have to visit the colony, we can go right now. I didn't mean to frighten you." Isla bowed her head in shame and Zennor copied her movements, trying to perfect the humanfolk's emotions.

Grandad Monty looked surprised. "You're tellin' me that if I jump in there I will become a mermaid?" He pointed his stick towards the ink coloured pool.

"Technically a merman," corrected Zennor.

Suddenly, Grandad Monty threw his stick into the air, and with a spectacular leap from his good leg he crashed unceremoniously into the freezing cold pool below. Zennor had to thrust her tail with all of her might to save herself from being squashed. Before Isla realised what had happened, Grandad Monty was nowhere to be seen.

Panic rising in her chest, Isla searched frantically with her eyes, shouting for her grandad; terrified that she had gotten this all wrong. Zennor was also nowhere to be seen, but just as Isla was ripping off her jacket to jump in, Zennor broke through the surface, followed by a very tiny, silver-haired merman, complete with a glittering navy coloured tail. It was Grandad Monty!

"Woohoo!" shouted Grandad Monty at

the top of his tiny voice.

Isla began giggling at his excitement, and Zennor joined in, playfully swimming in circles whenever Grandad Monty crashed back through the surface of the water. Isla clapped with delight and relief.

"Okay, now it's my turn," she whispered to herself, and with that, holding the book, she leapt into the water with a splash.

Just as before, Isla emerged from deep below the surface, spotting the blurry, sparkling tails of Zennor and Grandad Monty high above her. As Isla swam up, Grandad Monty and Zennor swam down to meet her halfway.

"Ready?" grinned Zennor. "On the way we will think of a story, so that we don't blow your cover... or mine! Here, we best hide that book, put it in my merpouch."

Isla had quite forgotten about the book and realised she was still holding a now miniature-sized copy in her tiny hand.

Zennor took the book and placed it into a little pouch made of seaweed which hung over her shoulder like a satchel.

The three swam off into the darkness of the cove and, as before, all of the twinkling lights extinguished themselves one by one.

CHAPTER 15

IN AN OCEAN FAR AWAY...

Meanwhile, many tides away in the heart of the Indian Ocean, a small merman was plotting his escape.

Along the trade route he would go; inside his cramped cage, he would sit patiently. The journey itself was treacherous; out in the open seas, merfolk were vulnerable to seasprites and all manner of deadly creatures. He didn't care. He would bide his time, monitor his captors, and keep a notebook of his observations. He was on a mission, and his goal? To reach Porthzennor Cove. It was only a matter of time...

CHAPTER 16

DARK FORESTS OF KELP AND
CREATURES

Along the way to the merfolk colony, Grandad Monty would not stop doing backflips, interchanged with rapid conversation and squeals of joy. Isla was beginning to feel exhausted just looking at him.

"Don't you think you should conserve your energy, Grandad?" asked Isla, exasperated by all the activity.

"Isla, I have not been able to expel energy like this for years! I feel like a young lad again. You would take that away from me, would ya?" He winked and continued his antics.

Isla sighed heavily and Zennor laughed at the pair of them.

"Okay, stop," hushed Zennor, pulling her companions close to her and into a sort of huddle. "We need to be very careful when we get there. Remember, you are travelling merchants from the Indian Ocean Trading Company. You came to sell... er..." Zennor glanced around, as if looking for inspiration. Then she remembered the book. "Stories! You are trading stories. Sometimes we do get those sorts of traders, but they tend to be a bit strange..." She cocked one eye at Grandad Monty as he listened intently.

Grandad Monty remained engrossed and oblivious.

"Thing is, it is compulsory for all official visitors to attend the seahorse academy to prove they are able to ride around the mercity. Like a sort of test."

Isla and Grandad Monty looked at each other with some trepidation.

"But we have never ridden a seahorse before," said Isla. "And that is one sentence I never ever thought I would say!"

Grandad Monty nodded his head in agreement; his expression seemed to imply that it was a fair comment.

"Ugh! Yes, I know, but I can teach you the basics, it's not *that* difficult. Also, we need to hunt you both a seahorse; you absolutely cannot show up without one. Goodness, there's so much to do, we best get going." Zennor started to swim forward, but Isla and Grandad Monty remained still.

"Er, Zennor... what do you mean we have to *hunt* a seahorse?" asked Isla, looking wildly uncomfortable with the whole idea.

Grandad Monty simply cocked his head at Zennor, giving her a curious look.

"Look, it really isn't so bad," pleaded Zennor. "There is a hunting ground in the kelp forests, not far from here. Why don't we go and have a look?"

Isla groaned at the prospect, looking to Grandad Monty for a voice of reason.

"Come on, pal. We've come this far. What doesn't kill you makes you stronger, ain't that right?" He held out a supportive hand to Isla, who took it and sighed.

"That's the thing, Grandad. It might very well kill us. Didn't you see the seahorses at the gates? There's no way we can catch one, let alone ride one!"

"Now that doesn't sound like my Isla," said Grandad Monty. "Where's your spirit, my girl? Come on, it'll be an adventure!"

Isla sighed again, and with much trepidation, they followed Zennor into the darkness of the kelp forest.

The forest was murky and foul smelling, like washed up seaweed that had been sat in the sun for too long. In the distance, Isla could hear the screeches and cries of some terrifying and unidentified creature; the tense atmosphere made her shudder with nerves. Holding their noses, the three merfolk swam deeper and deeper into the desolate, ink coloured forest. Eventually, they stopped beside a huge, gnarled tower of kelp. Behind the strands of weed before them were wild seahorses, grazing mindlessly on seagrass. Zennor pointed in their direction.

"Okay, there they are. Remember, they are wild, so you need to be very careful. First, you have to sing to them, to sort of hypnotise them. Then, once a seahorse has lowered its head for you, you climb onto its back and ta dah! They are yours and will remain loyal for life. I'll sing you

175

the song; you'll need to learn it, else you will never catch yourself a seahorse.

Where grey Land's End repels the sky,
The granite boulders stand,
Reared in a column. There they lie,
Laid by a giant's hand,
And there the ascending seabirds fly,
Beyond the last of land."

Grandad Monty had a small tear in his eye once Zennor had finished.

"Well I never," he said. "That's the ballad of Zennor, that is. It were on that paper you found stuck in my book, that day in the kitchen at the London house." Grandad Monty pulled at the bag around Zennor's shoulders, releasing the book. From beneath the front cover, he slipped out the piece of paper with the strange ballad, handwritten and faded with time.

"Grandad, the seahorses, look!" Isla

pointed to the strange, scribbled warning. "It says: *'when the song is done, the seahorses will bow and you shall be one'*. Someone else knows about this cove, Grandad!"

Everybody stared down at the note and Zennor looked confused.

"Why would anybody know about us? We have never had a visitor before, except via the trade routes." She looked as if she might cry.

"Don't worry, Zennor," said Isla. "Your cove is protected. This book is very, very old."

Zennor nodded slowly and returned the book to her seaweed pouch. Isla held onto the piece of paper and read through the verse one more time. She decided that she would go first, until Grandad Monty took the paper from her and strode confidently forward.

"I'll be the guinea pig, don't you fret, my

girl. I got no life to lose; done it all, you see," chirped Grandad Monty.

Before Isla or Zennor could protest, he snuck up behind a very large, regal looking seahorse, the colour of amber. The glorious creature had flecks of bright red and yellow on its body, and its silky mane was a deep terracotta. Isla felt very nervous for her old grandad, who could be attacked if it all went wrong and the seahorse rejected his song.

As softly and sweetly as he could, Grandad Monty sang his way through the first few lines of the song. Zennor and Isla waited anxiously, hardly breathing and hyper alert. The seahorse seemed to go into a trance-like state, bobbing very slowly on the spot and closing its piercing blue eyes. By the middle of the song, the seahorse very gently lowered its head, allowing Grandad Monty to climb carefully onto its back. The seahorse neighed affectionately and Grandad Monty finally let out a deep breath of relief. The seahorse glided through the water in circles, allowing Grandad Monty to get used to the feeling of riding him.

"You must name him!" called Zennor.

Grandad Monty scratched his head; he hadn't considered a name. "I'll call you... Coralcharge," he said. "On account of your coral colour."

"Okay Isla, now it's your turn – off you go." Zennor pushed Isla forward into the clearing, where a small blue coloured seahorse grazed.

This seahorse was the smallest Isla could see, so she decided it would be the best option for her. She didn't need a huge, regal horse like her grandad. Carefully, she mimicked what she had seen Grandad Monty do and crept slowly through the seagrass, getting as close to the beautiful creature as she could without startling it. The seahorse munched repetitively on the same piece of grass and seemed to be unaware of anything going on around it. Once Isla was within earshot, she began her song.

Unlike Grandad Monty's seahorse, this one didn't gracefully close its eyes. Instead, it began to throw itself around as if Isla were screaming a rock song at it, whipping it's head up and down riotously. Confused, but undeterred, Isla continued her song in a shaky voice. Once she had finished the entire song, the seahorse swam towards Isla and dipped its nose underneath her, flinging her so forcefully upwards that she was thrown into the open ocean, before floating back down and landing with a bump on its back. The seahorse began to canter around wildly in all directions, zig-zagging this way and that, making Isla feel quite sick.

"Name it!" cried a horrified Zennor from

behind a kelp tree.

"I-I... I w-i... will c-a... call you... Pipesnout!" stumbled Isla, as she was bumped up and down by the chaotic seahorse.

"Stroke its mane!" shouted Zennor, as the seahorse neighed in distress.

Isla began to shakily stroke Pipesnout's mane as gently as she could, while holding on with the other hand. Eventually, Pipesnout came to an uneasy stop, breathing heavily and swaying his head anxiously. Isla wasn't sure if he was about to throw her off his back and into the surrounding ocean. Finally, the wild seahorse started to relax and neigh gently back at Isla, giving in to her strokes and letting her sit comfortably on his back.

"That was a wild one, I have never seen that before!" giggled Zennor, emerging from behind her kelp tree.

Grandad Monty came gliding over on

Coralcharge, clapping jovially. "Well done, old pal! You did it!"

Grandad Monty was laughing and Isla couldn't help but let out a huge sigh of relief. She felt a glowing pride at her achievement, deep within her heart.

After much chattering and laughter about the unusual events, the three new friends swam back towards the mercity with their new seahorses.

CHAPTER 17

VISITORS FROM 'THE DRIFT'

Isla bumped up and down on Pipesnout as she became used to the seahorse's rhythm. She watched as Grandad Monty hummed merrily ahead of her, confident and happy on Coralcharge. Zennor held on to Pipesnout's mane and glided along next to Isla.

"Here we are," Zennor announced as the mermaid city became visible, its sparkling lights emanating through the currents. "We will keep your seahorses in the seahorse academy; they can live in my stable with my seahorse, Whipsydaisy.

Let's hope that nobody asks to see your seahorse skills today."

Grandad Monty and Isla nodded sagely and Grandad whistled to Coralcharge, who slowed down easily under his command. Isla tried to follow suit, but Pipesnout brayed his head and let out a rather long burp, sending a sprinkle of bubbles into the water in front of his little snout.

"Okay, as long as they won't mind..." replied Isla cautiously, as Pipesnout bucked up... again.

Zennor giggled and patted him on the neck. "He is a dear thing!"

Isla shrugged; she wasn't sure she agreed.

"Okay, when we get inside, just follow me. You two look like real merfolk now, so nobody will question you. We get lots of travelling merfolk coming in and out. If anybody does, you are here on behalf of the Indian Ocean Trading Company, doing official business with the royal family, okay?"

Grandad Monty smiled. "Aye, aye ma'am." He flourished his arms in a circular gesture and bowed his head.

Zennor beamed back. 'Exactly, good sir.'.

The three friends continued their path up to the gates. Merfolk of all colours and sizes buzzed about their day; folk music was playing somewhere inside the walls and merfolk were chattering away. They continued up the road, passing the market stalls as they had done before. Isla saw one stall selling delicate shell purses with every sort of spiral shape you could imagine, in every combination. The shells wove into each other in never ending patterns, spotted with flecks of pearl. She made a note to purchase one before she returned; her mum would adore such a trinket, and she could place it proudly with her own ornaments from her travelling adventures with Dad. Isla felt a rush of excitement at being able to add to her parents' collection from her very own wild adventure.

As the three glided through the masses, merfolk called out 'good morning, princess' to Zennor, who smiled regally and seemed to swim straighter. Isla followed suit; she was, after all, being escorted by a *princess*, though Isla kept forgetting this when it was just the three of them.

Grandad Monty, of course, did not take the slightest bit of notice, and responded with his own barrage of greetings, hardly letting anybody pass without a 'hello!', which made everybody smile.

Eventually they made it to the entrance of the seahorse academy, a rather grand building with big, heavy wooden doors, crusted with barnacles which gave it a look of being covered in armour. As they approached, the doors slowly opened and the darkness inside was revealed. Pipesnout decided that he did not like this and reared up violently, forcing Isla to hold on tightly, though she was becoming used to his unpredictable movements.

"Shh, it's okay, Pipesnout. Calm..." she said softly into his little ears, relaxing as he slowed his movements. Perhaps he was finally accepting his new role as her pet?

Grandad Monty rode past on Coralcharge and patted Isla on the back. "That's my girl, always so brave."

"This way, don't worry. It's always so dreadfully dark in here," called Zennor.

They continued forward and Isla couldn't see her hand in front of her face, it was so dark. She could hear the sounds of bubbles, snorting and a menacing flapping as the water around her began to grow warmer. *What's out there?* she wondered, feeling uneasy.

Magically, hundreds of torches lit up around them, enveloping them in bright light. Isla realised that they were in an aisle of stables, each one housing a beautiful seahorse, all of them cooing and blowing bubbles. A huge sense of relief washed over her as she realised that these were the bizarre noises she had heard in the darkness.

Zennor swam on ahead, while Grandad Monty leaned over the gates of one stable, stroking the head of a doe-eyed little seahorse who looked rather sleepy.

Once Zennor reached a golden-coloured stall, she turned to them. "Meet Whipsydaisy!"

Zennor opened the gate and out bobbed the most beautiful seahorse Isla had ever seen. She had a luxurious aquamarine mane which faded into a dazzling light blue. Her body was turquoise with sparkly flecks of silver, her eyelashes were long and thick, and her fins were translucent white.

Zennor nuzzled into her neck and Whipsydaisy blew an affectionate stream of bubbles. "Isn't she glorious?" cooed Zennor, stroking her seahorse friend gently down her long mane.

Whipsydaisy batted her eyelashes at Grandad Monty, who smiled and waved back, then at Isla, who left Pipesnout to go and stoke the beautiful creature.

"Oh, she is beautiful. Perhaps she can teach Pipesnout how to behave..." she threw an affectionate glance back to Pipesnout who bobbed up and down awkwardly with his mouth open.

"Right, let's put them all in with Whipsydaisy, she will help settle them in. Seahorses, once tamed, are very social creatures."

Grandad Monty confidently led Coralcharge into the stable and he entered politely with a bow of his head. Isla had to tug at Pipesnout to force him in. Eventually, after much defiance, Pipesnout relented, letting Isla and Zennor push him ungracefully into the stable where he bobbed and snorted angrily.

"He will learn eventually; sometimes they take some... adjusting," said Zennor carefully, trying to reassure Isla, who was panting with the effort and scowled back at Pipesnout.

Zennor secured the door with a brass key from her shell pouch and all three seahorses settled in.

Meanwhile, outside the stables, the piercing sound of conch shells being blown was causing chaos amongst the merfolk.

"Zennor, what is that awful noise?" Isla yelled, covering her ears.

All of the seahorses began to snort loudly and wildly.

Zennor looked shocked, her eyes wide and her mouth open. "Bandits! Bandits!" she squealed, grabbing Isla and Grandad Monty forcefully by the wrists, dragging them further into the seahorse academy and into a small side room, almost hidden by a huge shell. She began pulling desks and a cupboard in front of the door, which she locked in a flurry.

Isla watched, not knowing what to do or what was going on as Grandad Monty tried to help tip the other desks on top of the pile of furniture in front of the door. Now they were barricaded inside.

"What is going on, Zennor? Are we in danger?" stuttered Isla.

"The bandits... they come on the North Atlantic Drift; usually we are prepared for them. They try to steal our seahorses and our belongings. Sometimes they even take prisoners. Oh merwizzles, this is very, very bad!" Zennor swam in small, hurried circles, covering her ears.

Isla hurried over and put her arms around her to try to calm her down.

Grandad Monty called them both from below a small glass window, breaking the tension. He had upended a desk so that they could hide but still look out of the window at what was unfolding. Isla watched on in horror as merfolk screamed and darted into shell houses, coconut husks and anywhere they could hide. She saw a set of dark figures winding their way up the path through the market where they had just been, extinguishing lights as they went. Merfolk were screaming and scarpering, grabbing their children and fleeing at speed, leaving their belongings behind.

The menacing group of shadows continued in unison until Isla could make out distorted, pale faces, clearing a path as they went. Unlike the merfolk living in the cove, who sparkled every colour of the rainbow like sweets in a jar, these merfolk were every shade of darkness and sorrow you could imagine. They left a trail of ink behind them as they wove further through the marketplace, darkening the water around them midnight blue; strings of broken fins trailing behind them in the ink. Even Grandad Monty gasped at their menacing appearance.

They could make out at least fifteen of the bandits, if not more, and as they marched past the seahorse school and the little window, the three friends ducked behind the desk, just in case.

"They may try to break into the seahorse academy," stuttered Zennor in hushed tones.

"Those armoured gates looked very secure, Zennor, try not to panic," reassured Grandad Monty, but he did not take his eyes off the bandits.

"They seem to be heading towards the palace," said a wide-eyed Zennor.

As the bandits passed, a disgusting, toe-curling smell of rotting fish trailed after them, and the whole street filled with midnight ink. The bandits were singing a dirge as they marched: 'yo ho, yo ho, we will seize, plunder and go...' continuously in low, menacing voices, making the ground shake.

Isla noticed that some were dragging cages. "Zennor, what is in those cages?" whispered Isla, grabbing Zennor's hand and pointing in the direction of one of the cages.

"Oh no... no, no, no this is bad, bad, bad..." Zennor shook with fear. "They've taken hostages... they must have brought those poor merfolk with them as a threat to us."

Isla peered through the inky black and noticed specks of bright red inside one of the cages; the familiar translucent glow of a merfolk tail.

As one of the cages went by, close to the window, Isla felt a pull in her heart; a small tug that made her look again deep into the cage. There, she saw a pair of bright blue eyes, lonely and afraid, but alive.

Her heart stopped. Those were her dad's eyes. That was her dad's face; her dad's hair. She remembered cuddling into his chest as a small child; the smell of his coffee; his strong hands stroking her hair; her mother singing in the kitchen, happy and carefree.

She shook her head and tried to take another look, but she couldn't see the cage anymore. The procession of bandits had passed and were on their way up to the palace. Isla turned to look at Grandad

Monty, who was staring back in her direction, wide-eyed and muttering something under his breath, which Isla couldn't make out. One of the bandits at the back of the group threw something at the last market stalls in the row, laughing demonically with each hit. They watched helplessly as the stalls began to burn in blue flames.

CHAPTER 18

THE RESCUE MISSION

Once the bandits disappeared, the merfolk began to creep from their hiding places, frantically trying to extinguish the burning blue flames.

"Quickly, let's get out of here," said Zennor, tugging at Isla and Grandad Monty, who were still in shock. "You must go back; this is no place for humans," Zennor exclaimed as she pulled them towards the barricaded door.

Realising that it would take them hours to undo their hard work, she grabbed a chair and swung it high above her head, smashing it through the small window as tears began to fall down her cheeks.

Isla and her grandad looked at each other and Grandad Monty took Zennor gently by her arms, pulling her into his chest as she continued to sob. Placing his hands on her shoulders, he looked into her eyes, his wrinkled forehead crumpled in concern.

"I have been hobbling around on a stick for as long as I can remember, but today, I have never felt more alive, and that is thanks to you and your wonderful merfolk. If you think we going to leave you to deal with this mess all by yourselves then you've got another thing coming, my girl. We are at your service, ma'am!" Grandad Monty gave a theatrical bow and kissed Zennor on the hand.

Zennor began to cry in relief; she knew she needed all the help she could get. She gave them both a hug.

"I promise to protect you with all my power, but I cannot guarantee your safety," Zennor said, giving them both a serious look.

"Don't you worry, my girl. We're willing to take a risk to help you and your people, aren't we, old pal?" Grandad Monty winked at Isla and she nodded in agreement. Seeing that merman prisoner had brought back so many vivid memories of her dad and she knew they had to free him, if only to piece together this strange puzzle.

Once outside the window, the three brave friends swam behind a boulder, which gave them a good view of the palace without being seen by the bandits. The inky fog had lifted slightly, meaning they could see the palace gates clearly. Isla watched as the guards held their ground, their trident forks aimed outwards, warding off the invaders.

Without warning, the ink swept forward and engulfed the guards, rendering them all unconscious. They hovered sideways in the water as if in a trance, like discarded rubbish in the ocean. Isla heard Zennor gasp as she clamped her hand over her mouth and shook her head in disbelief.

"The sleep elixir… they have the power of the sleep elixir! They are more powerful than I imagined," Zennor whispered urgently, as though Grandad Monty and Isla knew what that was.

With the guards floating helplessly, the bandits continued through the gates and into the palace.

"We must find a way to stop them… follow me!" With that, Zennor swam off at high speed, up towards the left turret of the palace. Isla quickly followed, along with Grandad Monty. The three of them sped gracefully through the water towards the roof of the palace. Zennor dipped into a small window, which Isla quickly realised was her bedroom. All of Zennor's textbooks on humankind were strewn about the place. Zennor swam over to a large bookcase and delved inside, hurling books around her until she found the one she wanted.

"Aha!" she announced. "This is a book all about the bad merfolk of the world. I knew I had seen a picture of their inky magic somewhere before. These particular vagrants spend their lives roaming from the gulf stream to the North Atlantic Drift, catching and terrorising merfolk along the way. They have almost certainly come from the Gulf of Mexico... they collect octopi on their way north as they drift along the current, stealing the ink to make potions. It seems that the only way to defeat them is by creating a whirlpool, which can only done by extremely powerful merfolk, usually elders. Merfolk power intensifies with age, and we live for thousands of years so you can imagine…" Zennor looked up from the book with startled eyes, her hands shaking.

"Zennor, do you know how to make a powerful enough whirlpool to stop them?" asked Isla. "I mean, you made us into merfolk, surely that is something…?"

Zennor shook her head. "I have spent most of my life studying the humanfolk and magic associated with them; I kept skipping my bad merfolk classes so I never learnt the basic magic to defeat them. But I am sure my mother has it taken care of, right? She is an extremely powerful mermaid!" Zennor looked back and forth from Isla to Grandad Monty frantically, seeking reassurance.

Suddenly, a loud bang came from deep below them.

"What was that?" Isla gasped.

"Oh no… they are here; they are in the

great hall, just below us. We need to go and check out what's going on down there. If my mother is caught off guard then she may not be able to… quickly, let's go!" Zennor flung the book aside and sped off through her bedroom door.

The three swam rapidly down a corridor, lined with framed pictures of great merfolk, gilded in shades of silver and gold. Isla swam behind Zennor, trying to be as quiet as possible while shaking uncontrollably, with Grandad Monty at the rear.

Eventually, they came to a tunnel which spiralled downwards. Thankfully, all the lights had been extinguished in the panic. The three swam down very slowly towards the great hall, where the bandits were sure to be found. The great hall was where Zennor's mother, the queen of the merfolk, sat on her throne and conducted her daily business.

A light emanated through the water from the hall, and the three of them clung to the sides of the tunnel, listening and watching in the shadows.

"Oi, Bill! How do I look on this throne?" called one of the bandits to another as he lounged on the throne, tail slung over the arms casually while twisting a lock of matted hair.

The throne was made of large razor shells which spiked up in different directions, their conical patterns creating a piece of art. Small bits of sea glass decorated the seat and the whole throne shone in an ethereal light.

Bill burst out laughing and the rest began to chortle along with him. One of the terrible crew wrenched a torch off the wall and began to swish it around in different directions, pretending to be the queen.

"My dear subjects," proclaimed the

bandit in a squeaky, high-pitched voice, "I do declare that I am finished! Finished for good! Scarface..." The bandit turned to the throne and gave a low bow to the bandit sitting there. "... is the new master of this merkingdom!"

Scarface looked down at him disdainfully from his seat on the throne. An eruption of laughter filled the great hall once again.

"Enough seahorse play, you scoundrels!" bellowed Scarface, who was clearly their leader. "We may have taken Cornwall but there is work to be done. Once we have this here queen as a hostage, we will have leverage with the other merkingdoms. We will take them, one by one, until we own all the seven seas!"

The other bandits cheered menacingly and clanked on the bars of the cages, scaring the merfolk inside and sending vibrations through the water.

The three friends look at each other in the shadows.

"Where is my mother?" whispered Zennor.

They all scanned the hall, moving a little closer to the light to get a better view.

"There," said Grandad Monty under his breath.

He pointed to a floating figure with seaweed attached around her waist and a tiara of pearls upon her head. She was tethered to one of the cages and appeared to be unconscious.

"Oh!" squealed Zennor.

Isla had to clamp her hand over her mouth to stop her.

"What do we do?" whispered Zennor through Isla's fingers.

"We must make a whirlpool and send them away, Zennor. That's what the book said, isn't it?" replied Isla.

"Yes, we need powerful magic..." said Grandad Monty.

"Why oh why did I skip those classes... I always assumed I was safe in the palace, you know?" Zennor began to cry silently, and small crystal tears dripped from her eyes and crashed to the floor.

"Oi, what's that noise?" yelled Scarface, hushing the bandits to listen.

Again, Isla clamped her hand over Zennor's mouth and all three friends held their breath.

"Quick, hide in the crevices along the walls, they won't see us in the dark," whispered Zennor.

They spread themselves against the wall of the tunnel, folding tight into the gaps in the stone, trying to blend into the darkness.

"Go on, you useless cretins!" bellowed Scarface. "We need to rid this castle of merfolk once and for all!"

With that, the bandits scarpered, calling to each other:

"Let's go this way…"

"You go that way!"

"We will rid this palace of the vermin!"

Isla closed her eyes tightly. *This could be it… we could be found and tortured…*

She heard a couple of the bandits swim past in a flurry of bubbles and off up the tunnel towards the gallery corridor they had just swam down. She could imagine them entering Zennor's room and ransacking her precious books. Would they find the page left open about bad merfolk… would they find them?

"Come on pal!"

Grandad Monty's urgent voice sounded in her ears as he tugged her from the wall and down towards the great hall. They kept to the shadows, hiding in the seaglass chandeliers as they looked down at the great hall. Below, the cages rattled, and Isla's mother along with her advisors floated on seaweed tethers.

"It's clear of bandits... we don't have much time, let's go!"

Zennor whizzed bravely down to her mother while Isla had her own mission. She spotted the first cage, the one which housed the mysterious merman. Cautiously, she approached the bars. Inside it was dark and gloomy, the water stale.

She put her face to the bars and whispered, "Hello?"

There was a rapid movement inside and the swish of a red tail. A face appeared on the other side of the bars. There, in the tiny merkingdom, inside a magical cave, and in the most dangerous of circumstances, was her long lost father.

Isla gasped and flew back from the bars in shock.

"Isla?" called the man in the cage, his

voice croaky from disuse but still as warm and comforting as she remembered. "Isla? It can't be... is that you?"

Isla swam cautiously back to the bars of the cage and looked again. There he was... it was him...

"Dad?" she whispered, poking a finger through the cage and touching his mop of hair, overgrown and tousled.

"How did you find me, Isla? How on Earth did you find me? My darling girl..." He began to cry and Isla joined him.

"Dad!" she sobbed. "I thought we would never see you again! How...? How are you also here, in the merfolk world?"

"I was on a job when I disappeared. I have been trying to get back to Cornwall ever since. I was working in Belize, in Mexico... you remember I sent you that postcard? Anyway, we were diving in the blue hole – it is endlessly deep, Isla, you wouldn't believe it – and I got trapped down there. I was rescued by a miniature merman, who took me to his colony and made me into a merman myself, so that I could survive long enough to return home. Then, their merkingdom was attacked by these bandits, and I was captured. And now... well, here I am. I knew I was close, I could feel it, and when Scarface said we were in Cornwall I just couldn't believe it!' Isla's dad trailed off as Grandad Monty hovered into view.

"Dan?" Grandad Monty shouted, a little too loudly.

"Monty? Is that you? How on Earth..."

Before Isla's dad could finish his sentence, Grandad Monty was clinging to the bars of the cage, ripping with all his might.

"We need to get you out, son. Your Imogen... she's broken, my boy. We need you back!" Grandad Monty was struggling frantically to break the bars, but to no avail.

Isla turned to look for Zennor, who was cradling her unconscious mother's head in her arms and weeping silently.

"Zennor, Zennor! Help us, please! It's my dad... MY DAD!" called Isla desperately as Grandad Monty struggled.

Zennor turned, her tears glittering on her cheeks, and with an angry spin and whip of her tail a great shockwave spread through the hall. The chandelier wobbled violently, and shells dropped from the ceiling to the floor in great crashes. Suddenly, all the cages splayed open, freeing the captured merfolk who swam out dizzily. Zennor blinked and looked almost shocked at what she had done.

"Quick!" yelled Isla to the dazed merfolk. "We must hide!"

Grandad Monty gave a little whistle and suddenly a collection of bubbles emerged from the doorway of the hall. Instantly, Coralcharge was by his side.

"There's a good pal." Monty patted him grateful on the neck as Coralcharge stood proudly to attention.

Seconds later, Whipsydaisy and Pipesnout galloped regally into the hall, rearing and bucking at the sight of their masters. Isla cooed over Pipesnout and Zennor mounted Whipsydaisy, who stood to attention with pride.

"Quick, Dad, get onto the seahorse. Everything will be fine."

Isla helped her frail and weak father onto the back of Pipesnout as Grandad Monty loaded Coralcharge with other captured merfolk. As their seahorses hurried towards the hidden tunnel, Zennor began to tie her floating mother to Whipsydaisy's neck.

CHAPTER 19

A WONDROUS WHIRLPOOL

Isla watched as more black ink filled the water and spread out like a disease. A booming voice rose from the darkness as Scarface swam menacingly towards Zennor.

"Who do we have here then?" the bandit leader taunted.

Zennor jumped onto Whipsydaisy and tried to flee, but as she did so, she was caught by a whip of seaweed and restrained by four bandits. Whipsydaisy brayed and squealed in defiance, but she was no match for the seaweed and her captors. Zennor let out a cry of terror and it took all of Isla's might not to rush out to her help her friend.

"Ah, if it isn't the little princess... yes, we forgot about you. The wild child of Cornwall, isn't it? Doesn't listen to her teachers or her mother – we all laugh about you, the wayward daughter of such a *powerful* queen," jeered Scarface. "Your mother can't save you now little princess!" He laughed, followed by his comrades.

Zennor did not look afraid anymore; instead, she had her eyes closed and a frown on her face, as though she was concentrating. Isla couldn't work out what she was doing. Why wasn't she fighting them? Then Zennor began to move her lips, as if speaking to herself.

"Scarface, the cages! They're bust! The hostages have gone!" yelled one of the bandits.

Scarface growled and started to wind a

piece of seaweed around in circles, getting ready to throw it at Zennor. Suddenly, the waters around Zennor began to whirl, shielding her inside a small vortex, her hair cascading out into the current and whipping around her face. The waters were guarding her from the ink that was now flowing from Scarface's mouth in abundance. All the merfolk watched in tense anticipation from their hiding place.

"Scarface, what's happening? How can she do that? She is just a kid!" cried one of the bandits from behind their leader.

Scarface let out a louder growl and darker ink flowed. Eventually, the ink and the vortex of water met in a collision of energy. Isla could see through the whirling that Zennor's eyes were still closed tight, her mouth still muttering words.

"Grandad, she's doing it!" gasped Isla. "She's making the whirlpool!"

"I can see, my girl... I can see..." replied a stunned Grandad Monty.

The two powers were at odds with each other and, to the merfolk's dismay, the whirlpool began to lose momentum.

Scarface gave an almighty cackle. "Not so strong are you now, little princess! You are no match for dark magic!"

The bandits began to cheer in unison.

Suddenly, there came a powerful blast of cool, fresh water from the back of the great hall. Zennor was sent rushing backwards and hit the wall, and the bandits were scattered to all corners of the room. Isla, Isla's dad, Grandad Monty and the other merfolk dashed to hide once more. The clean water rushed in with such force that nobody could see what was behind its power. The ink dissipated and the bandits transformed into sickly-looking merfolk with pallid faces and weak tails.

In through the door now flowed shafts of white light, sparkling with flecks of silver, and a mermaid with black, glossy hair, eyes of sapphires and a tail that looked as if it were made from gold lace appeared. Isla gasped, along with the other merfolk. The beautiful mermaid floated through the great hall, a long, crystal trident in her hand, commanding all the attention in the room.

Isla looked for her friend and noticed Zennor slowly recovering from her dazed position on the floor.

The ethereal mermaid began to speak. "All you unsavoury creatures, swept up from the depths of the darkest oceans, what business brings you to this peaceful cove?" Her voice streamed out of her body like music, causing all the bandits to fall into a daze. She waved her stick and a whirlpool of water collected Scarface from his hiding place behind the royal throne.

"You beastly creature! Speak now to your creator and light bringer!" boomed the mermaid.

"We will leave... Your Highness... we want nothing from these good people, it was all a misunderstanding," mumbled Scarface, suddenly seeming a lot smaller and less frightening when held in the whirling water before the glowing mermaid.

"Misunderstanding? Pah! You take me for a fool, Scarface. I know exactly what you have been doing. I created the mercolonies to bring peace, and yet you... you and your tribe of villains would destroy the peace I have spent thousands of years nurturing. You will pay for this!"

With that, the mermaid twizzled her trident and pointed towards the ceiling of the great hall. Cages began to spring forth and, one by one, the bandits were sucked up into them and bars slammed shut before them, imprisoning them in the ceiling.

The powerful mermaid returned her attention to the bandit leader, baring her pointed teeth. "What say you now? The great Scarface of the Mexican Gulf?" boomed the Mermaid.

"I am sorry!" he quivered.

The mermaid laughed, and with a flourish of her trident, he too was sent to a cage high up in the rafters of the great hall. Suddenly, the entire room seemed to let out a breath.

The mermaid floated down towards Zennor, who watched with her mouth wide open.

"Princess Zennor, where is your beloved mother? Is she in danger?"

Zennor dumbly pointed towards her mother, entangled in the seaweed ropes, still attached to Whipsydaisy. The mysterious mermaid drifted to her side and laid her trident gently upon the queen's body. Slowly, the seaweed unwound itself, and the queen began to stir. After a few moments, she awoke, and looked about her, confused.

"Mother!" Zennor bolted to her side and engulfed her in an enormous hug.

Grandad Monty and Isla's dad held Isla's hand from inside the hidden tunnel.

"I think were safe, old pal," whispered Grandad Monty.

The strange mermaid lifted the queen's chin to assess her condition.

Finally, Zennor's mother spoke. "Morveren... you have saved us from peril. You are back in these waters again, always looking out for your people."

"Yes, my queen, I helped in your plight, but your brave little daughter is the real hero here. She singlehandedly took on the evil bandits. When I arrived, she was doing a good job with her own whirlpool, she just needed a little boost to keep her going." Morveren winked at Zennor, who blushed and bowed her head gracefully.

"We cannot thank you enough for your help, Morveren, but I was not alone. My friends helped to free the hostages from their cages and managed to get them to safety before the bandits returned." Zennor pointed towards the tunnel.

"Well, then we must meet these friends of yours," proclaimed the queen. "Come forth and show yourselves."

"It's okay Isla, Monty, come on out," called Zennor, still in her mother's arms.

Slowly, Grandad Monty and Isla revealed themselves from behind the door. Grandad Monty manoeuvred himself in front of Isla. She wasn't sure if it was to protect her or because he was eager to introduce himself to the queen and Morveren.

Confidently, he swam right up to Morveren. "The name's Monty. So, the legends are true, my lady..."He gazed directly into Morveren's eyes, his lips trembling.

"Do I know you, Monty?" asked Morveren.

"Aye, I dare say you may have seen me around these parts, I know all about you," replied Grandad Monty, a small smile forming at the corner of his mouth.

"And this is my good friend Isla," announced Zennor proudly, pushing Isla forward.

"I-I just helped... sort of... I suppose," blushed Isla, looking down at the floor.

Morveren took Isla's chin gently in her hand. "There is much bravery and adventure in this one... but she is not of this ocean. Tell me, child, from where do you hail?" asked Morveren.

"Ah yes, well, that is because they are both technically humans..." mumbled Zennor before she could stop herself.

"Humans?" shouted the queen in shock.

"Yes, well, I have been studying their kind for years and... I sort of bumped into Isla at the mouth of the cove... you know, where it is forbidden to go... and I thought I would try an incantation on her and it... it worked! I turned her into a miniature mermaid just like us! Can you believe it? All those hours of studying..." Zennor began to trail off as she registered the horror on her mother's face.

"I knew theoretically it was possible but I never... Zennor, you must teach me everything you know," commanded Morveren, to the surprise of everybody.

"But... we are not the only two humans here. My dad is here too. He was one of the bandit's hostages." Isla beckoned to her dad, who waited in the shadows of the room.

"Come forth!" called Morveren. "Do not be afraid."

Isla's dad slowly swam towards them, still weak from his time in the cage. Grandad Monty rushed to support him.

"And you were not turned by Princess Zennor?" questioned Morveren.

"No, my lady, I was turned in Belize, in Mexico while scuba diving. I got lost out in the open ocean while tracking illegal shark poachers. A kind merman saved my life and turned me into a merman so that I could find a way back to shore. That was when I encountered the troop of bandits." He looked up cautiously towards the ceiling cages.

"There are more with the powers of Zennor..." whispered Morveren to herself. "Zennor, you must accompany me. We must study this phenomenon together. Oh our wonderful world, how it is evolving," exclaimed Morveren to Zennor as she listened wide-eyed.

Zennor turned to her mother, who shrugged her shoulders.

"My little wild princess who could never settle into the ordinary life of the court. How could I forgive myself if I clipped your tail and did not allow you such a tremendous opportunity?" The queen said fondly. "My girl, you have studied hard and you must reap the rewards of your success. You shall travel the seven seas with the most powerful and revered mermaid of them all, the Mermaid of Zennor herself!"

Behind the, Morveren smiled.

"I promise I will not let you down, mother. What an adventure it will be!" exclaimed Zennor with a beaming smile on her face.

Everybody hugged each other and

there were smiles all around. Finally, the chaos was over.

CHAPTER 20

WE SHELL SAY GOODBYE

After they had eaten and rested together, telling their own stories of what had happened, Isla started to feel homesick for her own mother. She wanted to take her father home.

She tugged at Grandad Monty's tail. "Grandad, can we go home now?"

Grandad Monty smiled back at her. "I reckon so, my girl. I reckon so."

Zennor heard the exchange and embraced her new friends. From behind her, she pulled out a small shell purse which sparkled all the colours of the ocean. Inside the tiny purse was a wrinkled conch shell. Isla had ever seen one so beautiful.

"If you blow into this shell, no sound will emit, but I will hear you from wherever I am around the oceans of the world, and you can talk to me through the shell," explained Zennor to Isla.

"Kind of like a shell-phone?" giggled Isla in reply.

"A what? What is a shell-phone?" asked Zennor, wrinkling her forehead in confusion.

"One day, Zennor, I will show you."

Both girls grinned and embraced as new best friends.

Grandad Monty whistled and Coralcharge came to his side. Isla also whistled and, to her surprise and amazement, Pipesnout appeared. In fact, he seemed to have adopted an entirely new personality. The defiant creature now held his head regally and dipped his eyelids to Isla. In the background, she could see a small smile appear on Whipsydaisy's face.

"I told you he would sort himself out," winked Zennor, with a small nod to her trusty steed.

Isla could only image the battles that had occurred in the stables, and the lessons learnt.

Grandad Monty climbed onto Coralcharge and helped Isla's dad up to join him as Isla jumped onto Pipesnout. With many cheers and waves, the group of friends left the merkingdom. Merfolk emerged from their houses and out onto the streets, cheering, throwing coloured streamers and banging pots, shells and anything else they could find in appreciation of the efforts of the group. Isla watched as Grandad Monty waved regally; she couldn't help but have a little giggle at the sight. At the front of their procession was Zennor on the back of Whipsydaisy, only she did make quite a sight with her hair flowing behind her and her horse gliding gracefully through the streets.

Once they were outside of the gates, a band of guards wielding tridents accompanied them all the way back through the dingy, winding kelp forests and to the mouth of the cave.

Everybody hugged each other goodbye but they decided it was only a 'see you later'. They were now bonded for life after their magical experience, but it was urgent to get Isla's dad home and well again.

Zennor weaved her magic and, one by one, they returned to their normal size and back into their human forms at the water's edge.

Isla peered back down into the water at

a tiny Zennor. *How can something so tiny be so incredibly powerful?* she wondered.

"Go and take on the world, Zennor!" she said to her friend as they shared a last wave and goodbye.

Zennor called back, "Never be afraid, Isla. You are stronger than you think!"

With a final flip into the air, splashing them all with her tail, Zennor disappeared into the deep waters of the cave once more. With that, the adventure was over, for now. Isla had a feeling that her and Zennor would be having many more adventures to come. But for the moment, there was rest to be had.

Isla turned around to see Grandad Monty holding up her dad, stronger than before and without his stick, which was still discarded at the mouth of the cave. Her dad was looking rather poorly, with his head drooping slightly and little strength left in his limbs.

"Let's get him home, Isla," said Grandad Monty in a stern tone.

She could feel the worry in his voice and quickly ducked under her dad's other arm, helping to support him. The three of them struggled out of the cave and into the warmth of the afternoon sun. The beach lay stretched out before them, glittering and vast. The brightness stung their eyes as they squinted to see into the afternoon.

In the distance, a figure was running manically down the beach and toward them. It was Isla's mum.

"Isla? Dad? Where have you been? I've been beside myself!" she called out frantically as she stumbled her way towards them, tripping over the dimples in the sand.

She was too far away to see Isla's dad, as his hair covered his face.

"It's okay, love," called Grandad Monty.

Isla choked back tears. She couldn't leave her dad's side, otherwise he would fall to the ground, but she desperately wanted to run into her mum's arms.

As Isla's mum approached, she realised who the third person was.

"Dan?" she whispered, not quite believing her eyes.

Isla's dad looked up at her through his mop of hair. "Immy?"

"DAN!" Isla's mum cried, sprinting towards them and launching herself at Isla's dad, knocking him to his knees. She held him in a tight embrace, sobbing into his hair as she hugged him.

Grandad Monty pulled Isla into a hug as they watched her parents finally be reunited after all their time apart. Isla watched as the sadness that had hung over her mum evaporated in the afternoon sun, floating out on the breeze and away to the open ocean.

Finally, her family were back together again, and Isla couldn't stop smiling.

THE REAL STORY BEHIND 'THE MINATURE MERMAID OF ZENNOR'

The real Mermaid's Chair can still be found in the church in Zennor village, Cornwall.

The chair is still waiting for the mermaid to return to the church, with Matthew by her side...